HIGH SEAS HONEYMOON

High Seas Honeymoon

MADISON JOHNS

Copyright ©2015 Madison Johns
HIGH SEAS HONEYMOON
Madison Johns

All rights reserved.

In loving memory of my father, Dale Thayer

Cover by Susan Coils www.coverkicks.com/pre-made.html
Edited by www.ebookeditingpro.com
Interior Design by Cohesion Editing
www.cohesionediting.com

Acknowledgement

I'd like to thank the following readers, Martha Hawk, Patti Kinder Carroll, Lynda Bowles, and Carol Moury Sayres, for taking part in my birthday contest on my Facebook author page. They picked the cause of death for the victims in this book. Thanks for participating and I so appreciate your creative ideas.

High Seas Honeymoon

Agnes and Eleanor embark on a honeymoon cruise with their new husbands, Andrew and Mr. Wilson. There are plenty of other Tawas residents along for the ride, although the newlyweds don't realize this until they set out to sea. But the presence of the locals sets the stage for much drama to unfold ...

For instance, there's a crime ... Agnes and Eleanor find the body of a woman, but wait ... the body disappears before the ship's security and Captain Hamilton show up. To further complicate matters, there's a question of whether the woman was even really dead. But none of these details detour Agnes and Eleanor as they hone in on some very goon-like men, Ricky and Leo, to help them get to the bottom of what really happened. Will the women ever be able to figure out what really transpired, or will this be the one case they won't be able to solve?

PROLOGUE

I couldn't help but reflect back on the day I married my Andrew, and Eleanor also married her Mr. Wilson, in a double wedding at the lighthouse on the point in Tawas.

From the time Eleanor and I woke up that day, we had both hustled into the shower, taking our turns, of course. We stayed in our pajamas until the girls arrived to help us with our wedding dresses, and of course with our hair and makeup.

"Are the men here yet?" I asked.

"Don't worry, they'll be here," Elsie said.

"I know. I guess I'm having the jitters, and I haven't even written down my vows yet."

"Don't worry, the words will come when you're ready."

I fidgeted with the flower in my hair, and Elsie slapped my hand away with a brush. "Stop it or it will fall out."

My daughter Martha popped in, her eyes widening as she stared at me. "Oh, Mother. You're absolutely to die for."

"I'd rather not have dying mentioned today, if you don't mind."

"Oh, of course. The men are downstairs looking quite dashing, too. Just wait until you see Mr. Wilson in his tuxedo. I almost didn't know it was him."

I tried to visualize it, but couldn't, as my granddaughter Sophia came into the room carrying her baby, Andrea, who then said, "Nana."

My eyes widened in surprise. "She's talking now?"

"Yes, and she knows her nanas, it would seem. It's the only other word she's said besides Dada."

"That's typical for babies. I'm so happy that you're here, Sophia," I said, as I hugged her.

It wasn't long before the music began playing and the girls disappeared downstairs.

A minute after they left, Martha escorted us down the stairs that led from the lightkeeper's quarters of the lighthouse. About halfway down, my eyes met Andrew's, and my heart warmed. Eleanor whispered, "Doesn't Mr. Wilson look handsome?"

"Yes, very." And that wasn't a lie because he did. His hair was slicked back, and he had some actual color on his cheeks for a change.

I didn't have time to look around much more than that. All my attention was focused on Andrew.

Martha stood with us until Pastor O'Conner asked who was giving away the brides. "Me," Martha murmured. "Please take these ladies now," she said, dabbing at her eyes as laughter filled the room.

The pastor went through the typical marriage talk until it was time for us to read our vows to one another. Eleanor went first. "Mr. Wilson, you had me at your tuna casserole, really." Chuckles were heard, but she continued. "Never in my life have I met a man so caring and loving before. I'll love you all the days of my life, or whatever time we have left on this earth."

Mr. Wilson smiled. "I love you, Peaches, and I will until one of us draws their last breath. Thanks for consenting to be my wife, and I'll treat you like a queen, I promise. It looks like you already have your tiara."

"And Andrew?" the pastor asked. "Do you have vows?"

Andrew smiled as he took my hand. "I've loved you longer than you're aware. When you worked for me in Saginaw all those years ago, I looked forward to seeing you and enjoyed the coffee that you made special just for me. And after you quit, I thought about looking you up, but it never seemed the right time. From that day forward, I told myself that if ever you gave me a chance, I'd never let you go. You did, and I'm the luckiest man in the world. We might have our differences concerning your sleuthing, but I accept you for the beautiful woman that you are and I look forward to growing old together ... or old*er*." He laughed.

I gazed deeply into Andrew's eyes as I began speaking. "What can I say that hasn't been said? I'm so horrible at this, but I loved you at first sight, when I met you in Saginaw. I was a lonely widow, and you made me feel again, even if you never knew it. I kept my feelings to myself. Just seeing you every day at work was enough for me." I cleared my throat. "When you came to town, I tried not to feel anything for you, but I couldn't help myself. I fell in love with you all over again. You're kind, thoughtful, generous, and very, very loving. Thanks for picking me, my love."

The pastor finished speaking, rings were exchanged, and then he said, "Agnes and Andrew, Mr. Wilson and Eleanor, I pronounce you husbands and wives. You may kiss your brides."

Andrew took me into his arms, and as we kissed, applause echoed, followed by catcalls. When Andrew and I parted, I could see why. Mr. Wilson and Eleanor were French kissing, and his hands on the cheeks of her generous bottom.

I cleared my throat, and they parted. Our guests, who were packed tightly in the lighthouse, congratulated us. We left not long afterward amidst a shower of bubbles outside, as the rules said no rice was to be thrown. I gave hugs to my son Stuart, whom I had reconnected with not long ago, and his wife Moraine. When we parted, Stuart shook Andrew's hand, congratulating us. "It's your job to keep my mother out of trouble now."

"I'll try, but as you know, this is your mother we're talking about here."

We climbed into Eleanor's Cadillac, which was decorated with real flowers and tin cans tied to the back of the car, along with a sign that read, "Stand back twenty feet—senior citizens just married."

3

"Is that some kind of joke?" I asked Andrew.

"Probably Martha's idea of a joke."

We drove all through Tawas, honking the horn as we made it to Iosco Sportsmen's Club with Sheriff Peterson and Trooper Sales' squad car following us, with its flashers on and sirens blazing.

Chapter One

My mind snapped back to present when the fragrance of Andrew's cologne wafted over to me as I heard him approaching.

Andrew whistled as he walked into the room, picking up another suitcase, then leaving just as quickly as he had appeared. I'm Agnes Barton and I usually solve crimes in Tawas, Michigan, with my best friend Eleanor Mason. I married Andrew Hart on Christmas Day in a double wedding with Eleanor and Mr. Wilson, who is her new husband. Since it's winter, we decided to honeymoon out of town, somewhere much warmer. When Andrew first suggested that we go on a cruise, I was a little nervous. I've been know to get seasick on occasion and had heard that you still could even on a huge cruise ship, but I didn't want to tell him no when he had already bought the tickets. Eleanor was over the moon about going on a cruise and Mr. Wilson didn't care one way or the other.

I took my cat Duchess over to the Butler Mansion Bed and Breakfast yesterday. Mr. Wilson's granddaughter Millicent worked there and promised to take care of Duchess while we were on our honeymoon.

After Andrew had all of our luggage loaded into the car, we locked up and left.

Andrew squeezed my hand before he started the car, making way for Eleanor's house to pick up her and Mr. Wilson.

"Would you quit frowning? You should be excited about leaving for our honeymoon."

"I've just never been on a cruise is all. I guess I'm just a little nervous about being trapped in a boat for a week."

"Don't worry. It will be fine. Once we get down to Florida, you'll thank me."

I wasn't so sure, but I smiled all the same. We arrived at Eleanor's house ten minutes later, and she was waiting for us with her luggage already piled outside.

"Someone looks ready to go," Andrew said with a laugh.

I nodded. "I thought as much. Eleanor hasn't had the chance to travel all that much. Me either."

"Hopefully we'll have an uneventful honeymoon."

"Meaning *what* exactly?"

"Without a crime happening that you'll insist on trying to solve."

I laughed. "That doesn't happen all that much on cruise ships, does it? Of course I've seen a few news programs where someone on their honeymoon fell overboard." I gulped then. "You don't plan to off me on our honeymoon, do you?"

"I guess you'll have to find out when we're out to high sea." He winked.

Andrew got out and put Eleanor and Mr. Wilson's luggage in the trunk. Waiting until they got in the car, Andrew also put Wilson's walker in the trunk.

Then Andrew slid behind the wheel and headed toward the Iosco Count Airport. A young man at the airport helped load the suitcases onto the plane and we soon were all buckled in and the small plane was taxiing down the runway. Once we were airborne, I breathed a sigh of relief. I didn't mind flying, but in a small plane like this, you felt every turn. It was like being on a roller coaster and it made my stomach do summersaults.

When we made it to the airport in Detroit, we changed to a larger plane and had to go through the metal detector. Mr. Wilson set off the detector every time.

"What the hell," Wilson bellowed. "I don't have an Uzi up my keister, you know."

"Stop it, Mr. Wilson, before they strip search you," Eleanor said.

"I'd like to see them try."

"Didn't you tell me you were shot once?" Andrew asked Wilson.

"That's it. I have shrapnel in my leg. I completely forgot."

Needless to say, they did a strip search of Mr. Wilson and we waited until he came back with a huge smile on his face. "Teach them to strip search me. I made damn sure I farted good and long for them, too."

I smiled, but was thankful we were on the airplane without further incident.

Mr. Wilson and Eleanor were seated next to a dark-skinned man. "Are you—" Wilson asked.

The man interjected with, "I'm Hispanic."

"He's Hispanic," Wilson informed us from across the aisle.

"That's the politically correct name for Mexican," I said.

"Oh," he said. "Sorry," he told the man. "It seems I'm out of touch with all these new-fangled words. I try not to offend anyone. It's like when someone calls me elderly. Hate that word. It's like someone telling you that you're incapable of doing anything. I just got married to my Eleanor and I was quite capable on the wedding night, if you catch my drift."

The man smiled, obviously not taking offense. "You remind me of my papa. He always says exactly what he's thinking, too."

"There's no other way to be, in my opinion, but how did you know what I was going to say before I had the chance to say it?"

"I was searched by airport security after a lady told them I looked suspicious, so I figured others would think I'm a Muslim—not that there is anything wrong with that. I know plenty of nice Muslims."

"I was searched, too. I kept setting off the metal detectors and they wouldn't believe I had shrapnel in my leg," Wilson said, as he patted his leg.

The man just shook his head. "What war were you in?"

"None, actually. I had flat feet so they wouldn't take me; otherwise, I'd have been in the Korean War."

"Then how did you get the shrapnel in your leg?"

"I was a little careless with a firearm years ago, then there was that hunting accident when I was thirty. Ever been shot by a shotgun before?"

"No, thankfully."

"Well, I have some shot in me that couldn't be removed, the doctors say. It doesn't matter none to me, except when I'm going through an airport."

Mr. Wilson continued to chat the man's ear off and I had to chuckle to myself over that one. What was it with men and male bonding?

I took out my Kindle and began to read one of my many books. I often couldn't help myself when BookBub sent me those daily emails with bargain books. I'd almost become a book addict. I personally liked to have my Kindle read my books to me. It worked in a pinch when I didn't buy the audio books, which were much better with actual narrators. It took some getting used to, but I actually embraced all the new-fangled gadgets they had these days.

"It seems like Mr. Wilson and Eleanor are having a nice chat over there," Andrew said.

"You must mean Mr. Wilson. I don't think I have heard Eleanor say anything. They're such a sweet couple. I'm so happy that both Eleanor and I were able to find happiness. I'm still so shocked that I'm finally your wife."

"Hopefully in time you'll actually take my last name."

"I know, but I've been a Barton for so long it's hard to even think about changing my name. Please, give me time. I'm sure I'll sort through it soon."

"You could be Agnes Barton Hart if you'd like."

This wasn't the conversation that I wanted to have as we headed on our honeymoon. "Whatever you would like, Andrew."

"It's not like that. I don't want to tell you what to do at all. I hardly expect that you'd stand for it, anyway."

Andrew really had a valid point there. I felt bad that I was stalling about the name change. What really was my problem with it, anyway?

I didn't read for very long before I dozed off, and I woke with a start as the plane jumped a bit. "What's going on?"

"Just a little turbulence," Andrew said. "Did you have a nice nap?"

"I did. I can't believe I dozed off like that."

Andrew smiled. "I took a picture while you slept. I'll show it to you later."

"What was I doing that was so funny that you'd risk pulling out your cell phone? You're lucky the air marshal didn't come back here."

"What air marshal?"

'That man sitting up there," I said.

"You mean that portly man with a Hawaiian shirt on?"

"Exactly. Look how he's restless and keeps watching everyone who passes him to use the bathroom."

Andrew nudged me. "You want to be part of the mile high club?"

"The what?"

"You know, it's where we'd go into the bathroom together and—"

"Get freaky," Eleanor said from her seat.

I stiffened now at the mere suggestion. "The only thing I'm lowering my pants for in that bathroom is if I hafta pee."

"Uh-oh, Agnes. You know every time you say that you have to go for real," Eleanor said.

Sure enough, my bladder suddenly felt quite full. "I'll have to hold it somehow. The keep your seatbelt sign is on."

"Probably on account of the turbulence," Eleanor said.

Twenty minutes later, after much leg crossing, I had to get up and use that bathroom or else I'd be going right here. I unhooked my seatbelt and headed to the bathroom.

A stewardess met me halfway, telling me, "You need to sit back down."

"I can't. I hafta pee and if I don't do it soon, I'll be doing it right here in the aisle. I'm sure you'd rather not have the mess to clean up or the aroma for the rest of the flight."

"Good point, but hurry up."

The sign went off and another stewardess said, "The captain just gave us the all clear, Donna."

Donna smiled and headed back to the front.

I nodded as I passed the man wearing the Hawaiian shirt. "Good to know you're here?"

"Who, me?"

"You're an air marshal. I know you must be, with the way you keep watching all of the passengers."

"You're mistaken, lady. I'm just a passenger, like everyone else."

"I'm an investigator back in Tawas where I live and I'm quite observant."

"Good to know, but if you don't mind, I'd like to get back to my newspaper."

"I thought you had to pee," Donna said.

"No need to be cross with me. I bet your mother is very proud of you, the way you talk to senior citizens, I mean."

"I wasn't being rude, just reminding you is all."

"I don't need to be reminded, young lady, about what I came to the front of the plane to do."

"You're going to make the other passengers nervous."

I stared at the sweat on Donna's brow now. My bet was that I was dead on about her mother, or else she's just not accustomed to meeting someone like me. I decided to ease up on her before we were evicted from the plane at the layover.

"Sorry. I never meant to do that, just wanted to chat with this man here. If you'll excuse me, I'll use the bathroom and go back to my seat."

I finally went to the bathroom door and thankfully it wasn't occupied, so I squeezed into the tiny bathroom. It was so weird inside the tiny stainless steel compartment. I pulled my pants down and sat on the small seat that would be a problem if you were of a larger size.

When I stood, the door suddenly opened to my shock and a young man stared at me with wide eyes, very wide eyes! "Oops, looks like I forgot to lock the door," I said, not knowing what else to say. The door was slammed shut and I quickly washed my hands in the small stream of water that came out in the sink. Luckily I had handy wipes in my purse, which I quickly used, and then I came out the door, trying not to make eye contact with the young man who was waiting outside. After all, he'd already seen far more of me that he wanted to, I thought.

I finally slid back into my seat.

"What took you so long?"

"I was chatting with the air marshal up there, but he denied being one. Then I used the bathroom and flashed someone."

"What fun. Anyone I need to be aware of?" Andrew asked.

"No, just a young man."

Andrew laughed now. "He's scarred for life?"

"Most likely. That bathroom is so tiny that I hope Eleanor doesn't have to use it. That seat is made for a child, I swear."

I went back to reading and once again was woozy enough to drift off to sleep. That's about how it went for the rest of the flight. I never did find out if the man wearing a Hawaiian shirt was an air marshal, but when we arrived at our destination in Orlando, Florida, he was the first to leave.

"Why are you staring at that man?" Eleanor wanted to know.

"I thought he was a air marshal."

"And?"

"I never found out. I guess it doesn't matter now."

Mr. Wilson's walker was brought over by the stewardess and soon he was rolling up the aisle as we made our way from the plane and into the airport. We spent the next hour trying to locate our luggage, or my bag. "There's one with a paisley pattern," I said.

Andrew pulled it off and said, "It's missing the tag."

"It must have fell off," I reasoned with him. "Grab it so we can leave or we'll be late for the departure."

He gave me a strange look, but complied.

We left the airport and took a taxi to the port where the Matron Queen was waiting for us to embark on our honeymoon.

"Where did you say the ship was headed, Andrew?" I asked. I hadn't paid close enough attention to the details of our honeymoon since Andrew was happy to make all the arrangements. I'd much rather have gone to an all-inclusive resort, but in truth, I was just happy to be going anywhere that was away from the cold Michigan weather. I loved living in Tawas, but could have done without the winter weather.

"Cozumel and Costa Maya, Mexico, and also Montego Bay, Jamaica."

"I've never heard of any of those places, except for the countries. Have you been to them before?"

"Nope, I wanted to take you somewhere neither of us have been. That way it will be all the more special. I want us to create our own memories. The ship we're going on caters to the older population, too, for the most part."

"Now isn't that sweet," Eleanor said, dabbing at her eyes. She gazed over at Mr. Wilson. "I do worry about how Mr. Wilson will get around on the cruise ship. It seems like too much walking for him."

"Don't worry about me, peaches. Andrew and I have already hashed that out. He's renting me a scooter."

"As in, an electronic scooter where you can whiz around?" I asked, shocked. To me, this certainly didn't sound safe — for the other passengers, that is.

"Yup."

I forced a smile now, and said, "Sounds great. I'd hardly expect you to be able to walk around with your walker the entire time. I just hope you don't get lost."

"We all have cell phones," Andrew reminded me. "That way if we get separated, we'll be able to find one another."

When we arrived, at the cruise port the taxi driver took our suitcases out of the trunk and Andrew made a call on his cell and soon a young man met us, loading our luggage onto a cart that he had brought with him. "I have the scooter waiting for you."

After we checked in, Mr. Wilson hopped on the burgundy scooter and was directed toward the ramp. He rolled up it as we followed, taking care as we held onto the handrail. It was a much easier way than climbing all those stairs. From the looks of it, most of the senior-aged passengers also chose the ramp.

I gulped as I gazed up at the tall ship, which looked bigger than I had expected, with the many portal windows that told me there were many upper levels to this ship, not to mention how many lower levels there might be.

Once we were on the ship, Mr. Wilson slowly moved his scooter along and I stared up at the glass elevators with a gulp. I was scared to death of heights and I could already see this would be a challenge for me.

The cart was pushed into the elevator and we followed. Andrew whispered in my ear, "Relax, Agnes, you're white as a ghost."

"You know how I have a fear of heights."

Andrew took my hand in his and gave it a squeeze. "Just close your eyes, or better yet, bury your head in my shoulder. I think I'd like that."

I did just that as the elevator moved upward. "She's afraid of heights," I heard Andrew explain.

"Ah, she's not the first, but it's a great view on the way up, I understand."

I felt the rush that went over my head that usually happened whenever I went more than two floors up and I gripped Andrew's hand tight, until he said, "Ouch."

I loosened my hold on him and the elevator came to a smooth halt. Andrew put his hand on the small of my back and led me out into the hallway. Only then did I exhale. I was just glad I was out of that elevator. We walked halfway down the corridor and the door to our stateroom opened. "This one is your room, Mr. Hart." The young man took our luggage inside and he then took Eleanor and Mr. Wilson into the next stateroom and only after they went inside did I go into ours.

Once we were alone in our room, I fingered the soft beige comforter as Andrew set our suitcases on the bed. I opened a curtain on the wall, but only bare wall was on the other side. "Looks like we don't get a portal window after all. I can't say I'm upset about that. It's hard enough for me to know I'm five decks up."

"How do you know that when you had your eyes closed the entire time we were in the elevator?" Andrew laughed.

"I counted the dings as we passed each floor."

"Very observant, but I'd expect no less from you."

I checked out the bathroom and found a nice-sized toilet with safety rails next to it. The shower was open and handicapped accessible. The vanity counter was smaller, but would suit our needs. At this point I was a little tired and went back into the room as Andrew was unpacking his suitcase.

"I'm so tired," I said.

"I know, but we really should get on deck and watch our departure. It's an experience we shouldn't miss."

"I thought you said you've never been on a cruise ship before?"

"I meant I've never been to our destinations, dear."

I smiled and we went into the hallway and knocked on Eleanor's and Mr. Wilson's door. When they didn't immediately open up, I wondered if I was interrupting them at an importune moment, but instead Mr. Wilson came up fast in his scooter. "It's about time you two joined us. Hurry up before we miss the ship leaving."

We followed Wilson to the deck, where Eleanor was standing near the handrail. The horn sounded as the ship slowly moved down the channel that led to the great Atlantic Ocean.

Andrew drew me into his arms and gave me a passionate kiss, until Eleanor cleared her throat. "Cut it out, you two, you're gaining an audience."

Sure enough, as we broke from our embrace, we saw that a child of about eight was staring up at us, until his parents quickly told him to quit gawking.

I didn't give the boy much attention now, as the view was breathtaking. Blue ocean spanned as far as the eye could see. Our ship wasn't the only cruise liner leaving either. Princess, Carnival, and Royal Caribbean also had ships that were headed out to sea.

I breathed in deeply of the salty ocean breeze that was combined with my Andrew's cologne. Life simply couldn't get better than this. I was married to the man of my dreams and I was more than eager to enjoy our honeymoon without the usual distractions, like a crime wave happening.

Chapter Two

Once land had all but slipped away leaving barely an outline of the shore, we wandered along the deck. Familiar musical laughter was heard one deck below us and it stopped me in my tracks. "That sounds an awful lot like Martha's laugh," I told Eleanor.

Eleanor glanced away a little too quickly now.

"What gives, old girl?"

"Oh, just that I might have told her what ship we'd be on."

"You didn't? Tell me you didn't."

"What's the problem? With a ship this big I highly doubt we'll even run into her, even if she is on the ship," Andrew said. Then he frowned. "Although it would have been nice not to run into anyone we know here. I wanted our honeymoon to just be the two of us, or the four of us."

"Let's head down to that deck. I just have to know," I insisted.

Mr. Wilson motored down the deck as we followed.

"Slow down, Wilson," I said. "We can't keep up with you."

"I know. This is going to be a great cruise. Look at me cruise now." He zoomed toward a couple, causing the man and woman to jump out of the way just in time. They both landed on the deck with a slap of palms. Ouch, is all I could think.

"Sorry," Eleanor said. "He's not used to driving one of those things."

"They need to do something about him before he injures someone," said the man who fell, as he climbed to his feet.

We quickly scurried past, not wishing to converse with the

man further just in case he actually made a complaint. I hoped that wouldn't happen since this cruise was barely underway. It usually took us longer to get under someone's skin. Then again, perhaps not, I laughed to myself.

Once we were in the elevator and the button was pushed for the fourth deck, I felt a little better that we were going down and not back up. I had been worried that I'd feel a little seasick, but so far, I barely noticed the motion of the ship.

"I hope you're not planning to start anything with Martha, if she's really on this ship," Andrew said.

"I'll try not to, but there is just no reason she needs to be on this ship, the same one we're on. I'd love to know how she could even afford to be here since she barely works."

"Her jewelry business it really taking off," Eleanor said. When I frowned, she added, "Don't blame me."

"Well, you did tell her what ship we'd be on. It wouldn't surprise me that she's here, since we try to ditch her every chance we get."

"Ditch her? She doesn't hang out with us all that much. If she's here, it's for one reason, to find her some hot, younger man to hook up with."

"She does that regularly enough in Tawas."

"Yes, but it's not summer back home now, is it?"

"Good point." Eleanor was good at stating the obvious, which sometimes irritated me. I guess we both like to push our weight around at times. While I consider myself the leader of our investigating team, the truth was I'd be lost without Eleanor, but I'd never let her know that. It's just the way we get along. We love each other to death, but have no problem telling each other exactly what we think.

As the elevator doors opened, I said, "Now, Wilson. Take care now that you don't run over anyone else. This deck is mighty crowded."

"I didn't run the last people over, they dove out of the way. You can hardly blame me for that. If they were decent, they would have moved out of the way for a handicapped man who needs to use a rolling jalopy."

I decided to let this one go and Eleanor positively beamed at Wilson's wit. This round Wilson won and I was just happy that he drove at a reasonable speed now as we made our way up the deck.

As we drew close, I saw that Martha was indeed lounging on a chair, wearing a teeny tiny, yellow bikini. She put her hand over her eyes as she gazed up at me. "Could you move out of my sunlight? Can't you see I'm trying to get a tan here, Mother?"

"I'd love to tan you all right. What are you doing here, Martha?"

"Same as you, I suspect. Except for the honeymoon part."

"And you had to hop on the same cruise as us?"

"Well, there did happen to be a planned trip for those folks from the Sunrise Side Lifelong Learning. So I hijacked my way onto it, since they had a cancelation at the last minute."

"Cancelation, how exactly? I sure hope you haven't done something out of the way just so you could get aboard this ship."

"Look, I'm not like that. It's not my fault that the woman had to stay home. She had a waterline break. That'll teach her to keep her heat on fifty-five all the time. It's winter in Michigan, you know."

"Fine, but how about you stay on your deck and we'll stay on ours?"

"Sounds like a winner to me, except for dinner and most of the activities. Just pretend you don't see me."

A woman made her way past with four other women, who were just as dainty as the leader of the pack. They giggled as they passed and Martha informed us, "Wedding party."

"As in getting married aboard the ship?"

"Yup. Seems that Liz thought it would be a great idea. I haven't met the groom yet."

"Liz?"

"Yes, the bride. I met her in line when we checked in."

"Nice to be young and so much in love."

"Or old in love like us," Eleanor added with a smile.

I glanced around. "Where are the rest of the girls from your group?"

"Not sure, since I so lost them. I have my own plans for this trip and it doesn't include hanging out those old birds the entire trip. They have an entire agenda we're expected to be participating in as a group, you know."

"Old? You do know you're no spring chicken yourself. Your daughter Sophia is all grown up and you have a granddaughter, too."

"I know, but I'm not about to let that weigh me down. I'm just not that type of woman. I don't plan to ever act my age."

"Just like us, Agnes," Eleanor said.

I so wish Eleanor hadn't said that, since Martha grinned now. She really didn't need any encouragement to behave more badly than she already does. Back home, she wears catsuits, and that's hardly a fashion that is considered okay these days. She did have one thing going for her, and that was that she had a killer body for a woman over forty, which obviously helped her lure in the younger men.

My eyes widened as I stared down the deck. "Hey, isn't that Denise Munson from that club you came with?" I asked Martha.

Martha slid a little lower in her seat now, snatching a newspaper close by and pretending to read it, but I so wasn't having any of that.

"Hello, Denise, over here." I waved frantically to assure myself that I got her attention.

"Thanks a lot, Mother," Martha spat.

Denise strode over with a clipboard in hand. "Hello there, Agnes. I'm a little worried. Your daughter Martha is part of our group and I can't seem to find her anywhere. I sure hope we didn't leave her behind in Florida, but I was sure she came onboard."

"Not to worry, Denise. Martha is right here." I pointed her out.

Denise put a hand to her chest. "I'm so glad." She then eyed Martha's bikini when she set the paper down. "Well, it seems like you're catching a little sun, but we were going on a tour of the ship. Captain Hamilton was going to give us a tour of where all the action happens."

"In the casino?" I asked.

"No, I meant of the bridge."

"You mean where they steer the ship?" I asked. "I'd love to do that myself."

Denise smiled. "You can come along with us. If you can talk your daughter into putting a little more clothes on."

"What's wrong with what I'm wearing?" Martha asked, as she stood.

"Do you have to make a spectacle of yourself everywhere you go, Martha?" I asked.

"Whatever happened to you stay on your deck and I'll stay on mine?'

"You certainly wouldn't begrudge me the chance to see the bridge, would you?"

Martha picked up a sundress from the back of her chair, putting it on now. "And listen to you complain the entire trip? Not a chance."

Andrew smiled. "Go on, girls, I'll keep Wilson busy while you're gone. Just give me a call when you're finished."

"Sure, thanks, honey." I gave Andrew a quick peck, and Eleanor did the same for Wilson.

Martha followed Denise and we trailed behind them as they joined their group. My eyes widened when I spotted Leotyne Williams amongst them. "What on earth are you doing here, Leotyne?"

"Can't a gypsy take a vacation without everyone staring or asking why?"

I noted that she wore her usual all-black dress and her witch-like shoes on her feet. "I'm sure it has nothing to do with your apparel."

"Yeah," Eleanor added. "Aren't you hot in that dress?"

"No, I'm rarely hot."

"I just hope that I don't bump into anyone else I know here. So far this is the strangest honeymoon ever," I said.

"Pretty soon it will be right up you alley," Leotyne said.

I had to wonder now what she meant, but with my dealings with Leotyne, you just never knew what she was talking about. Ever since she had rolled into Tawas that time I was living at the campground for a spell, I quickly found out that she considered herself a fortune teller. I guess it came with the whole Romanian thing. Anyway, every time she shared anything with me, it was always in the way of a riddle as a direct warning.

I smiled in greeting at the four other women in their group. They introduced themselves as Ruby, Pearl, Violet, and Lenore.

"Nice to meet you ladies."

"Didn't you gals just get married?" Ruby asked, rubbing a hand over her unusually long facial hair that was over her lip.

"Yes, but Denise told us we could check out the bridge with you."

"Hardly seems fair to me," Pearl said.

"Now, ladies, let's be nice," Denise began. "We're all from Tawas and as such, we need to all get along. It's not like they're going to all of our activities. They're on their honeymoon."

"I didn't mean it exactly that way," Pearl said. "But we paid to get extras on our trip."

"Not to worry. Everyone in the group will have plenty of opportunities to do some exciting activities while we're here, like tonight, when we have dinner with the captain."

Eleanor frowned now. "Lucky ducks," she said.

I nudged Eleanor. "Now don't make them feel bad."

"I wasn't. I'd just love to have dinner with the captain, too."

"I'm sure you will at some point," Martha said. "You girls are good at getting what you want."

My brow raised as I said, "I think you might be speaking about yourself, Martha."

"No need to get into a family argument over this," Denise said. "We better head to the bridge now or we'll be too late."

Eleanor and I followed the pack of ladies that had paid for the privilege to see the goings on at where they steer the ship. I didn't like how some of them had made us feel like we didn't belong, but I decided not to let that bother me.

We were soon on the elevator going down, and each floor we passed made me feel a whole bunch better. On the main deck, we weaved our way to where a gold door stood with a portal window to look out. Denise pushed a doorbell of sorts and door was promptly opened by a young man wearing an all-white uniform with gold shoulder patches that signified he was the captain.

"We're here from the Sunrise Side Lifelong Learning for our tour," Denise said.

"Of course. I've been expecting you."

We walked inside and there was a beautiful sight of only blue ocean ahead. I marveled at all the new-fangled buttons and levers. I pressed a hand to my chest and asked, "Who's steering the ship?"

"It's on autopilot. We usually do that once we're out to sea," the captain explained. "I'm Captain Hamilton, and these are my navigation officers, Theo and Gunner Flynn. They're twins and they watch over the bridge so I can do my other duties, like making sure things are running smoothly and speaking with the passengers."

Eleanor beamed. "Like inviting some of them to have dinner with you?"

"Yes, I expect you ladies will be dining with me tonight."

"Not them. They're not part of our group," Ruby said, giving her gray hair a pat.

"I'm sure we can make room for them."

"We're actually on our honeymoon," I said. "And that would have to include our husbands."

"Perhaps another night, tomorrow?"

"Sounds like a plan," Eleanor said.

I half expected Eleanor to stick her tongue out at Ruby and was almost shocked when she didn't. I was happy that she was acting decent in front of the captain, at least.

Eleanor walked over and asked, as she poised to move a lever, "What does this knob do?"

"Don't touch that. It sets off the alarm that the ship is about to sink," Captain Hamilton said with a wink.

"You seem awfully young," I said. "Exactly how old are you?"

"Thirty-five. I've been on cruise ships most of my life. My father was a captain on the Princess line. You could say that cruises are in my blood."

"I'm Agnes and this is my friend Eleanor," I said.

"Nice to meet you ladies."

Denise, not wanting to be left out, introduced the others in the group. Martha then saddled up to the captain and took hold of his arm. "Are you currently single?" She laughed.

"Very single, but I have a firm policy to never become involved with any of the passengers. It makes for smoother sailing." He then laughed at his joke.

"That must be hard to do with all the passengers running around half dressed," Eleanor said. "Aren't you ever tempted, even a little?"

"It's natural to be, but I just don't look at anyone on this cruise ship in that way. Women weren't put on earth to be sexualized. I respect women."

"He must be gay," Eleanor whispered in my ear. "So, this ship is safe, then?" Eleanor asked.

"Very. I've never had a cruise where anything happened out of the way, even with passengers. Sunburn is the extent of it."

"No icebergs this far south either," Theo said.

I turned my attention to the navigation officers now. Both of them were blond and quite striking. From Theo's sight accent, I wondered if they were from Denmark possibly.

"Good to know," I said.

We listened as the captain grabbed a microphone and detailed the emergency procedures to all of the guests. He then showed us what each of the buttons and gadgets were. I noticed a panel along one wall with many red and green flashing lights.

"What is that?"

"It's our mainframe computer. The ship is run by it unless we get near to port and then I take over and steer the ship in."

Eleanor and I excused ourselves after the captain went into specifics about the ship that made me yawn. I didn't need all of those details to enjoy the trip. I'd much rather catch up with Andrew and Mr. Wilson.

Chapter Three

I called Andrew several times before he answered and he told us that he'd meet us in the atrium, where the crew would be doing the welcome aboard announcement. Eleanor and I wanted to go back to our rooms to use the bathroom before we met our husbands. It was hard not to hear the music that rocketed through the ship.

"Wow, that sure is loud," Eleanor said.

"I'd have to agree with you there," I said, as we came off the elevator and into the corridor that led to our rooms.

We hadn't walked all that far when we heard what sounded like something, or someone, hitting the wall at the end of the corridor. By the time we made it to where we heard the sound, there on the floor was a woman with a white towel around her neck. Part of the towel was formed like it was one of the ones that were left on the beds in the shape of a swan.

"Check that door, Eleanor," I said, as I knelt and checked the woman's pulse.

Eleanor opened the exit door and glanced down the stairs, coming back to me and dragging me off toward her room. She jingled the key in the lock and we were barely inside when we heard footsteps in the hallway.

"Great, I was hoping nobody would be up here," a man with a deep voice said.

"Hurry up, then, and be quick about it. The last thing we need is for someone to come up here and interrupt us," a man said.

"I'm going as fast as I can," came the man's response.

"Interrupting them doing what?" whispered Eleanor.

I gave her a look instead, as I could hear someone walking past the door. We waited until we could no longer hear the men in the hallway and then called downstairs, asking for help, and said that we had found the body of a woman.

Tears burned the back of my lids and I felt helpless until someone knocked on the door, alerting us that they were security. I opened the door and we moved into the hallway. Even though my eyesight wasn't the best, I could see that there was no longer a body on the floor.

Eleanor made her way down the hallway with security, and the captain showed up next, in what was now a crowded hallway with ten more security personnel. "What happened?" he asked us.

"We thought … we heard—"

"What my friend is trying to say," Eleanor began, "is that we found a body of a young woman with one of those swan towels wrapped around her neck."

"Then where is this body, now?" Captain Hamilton asked.

"I don't know, but it was there, I swear," I said. "I even checked her pulse and I didn't feel one."

"So what did you do then?"

"I checked the stairwell and could have sworn that I heard someone on the stairs," Eleanor said. "Whoever it was had to be coming up after us. That's why I came back in here and Agnes and I barely got into my room before we heard the voices of two men in the hallway."

"They were looking for us. And one of the men told the other to hurry. That must have been when they removed the body," I observed.

"So you never actually saw anyone on the stairs for sure?" Hamilton asked.

"No, but it's obvious they were after us since we did hear the sound of two men's voices immediately after we closed the door to my room," Eleanor said.

The security personnel gave the captain an amused look.

"We take false reports seriously," the captain said.

"But it's not false," I insisted.

"Then where is the body, or the towel?"

"How would I know? But we both saw the same thing. Perhaps you should check the cameras before you call us out for being liars."

"We'll check the surveillance tapes, but until then, stay quiet about this incident."

"Don't you want to know what the victim looked like?"

"Go ahead," Hamilton said.

"The woman was young and brunette," I said.

"But we didn't recognize her," Eleanor added.

"How would you, when this is a cruise loaded with passengers that you shouldn't be able to recognize unless you knew them from the mainland?"

"Well, you have a point, but it's not anyone we know personally, is what I meant to say."

Captain Hamilton just shook his head at us.

"No need to look at us like that, captain. We're not lying and you'll find out when you look at those tapes," I insisted.

He didn't respond and we agreed that we'd keep what we'd found to ourselves until he had the time to investigate the matter. I could tell by the way his eyes narrowed that he didn't believe a word of what we said.

After security and the captain left, we took a quick pit stop in my room to use the facilities. I sank onto my bed. "I can't believe this is happening. Death follows us no matter where we go." I sighed.

"Now, that's not fair, Agnes. How were we to know that a passenger would be murdered here on this ship?"

29

"But nobody but us believes that anyone was murdered."

"Good point, but we'll have to just investigate the matter ourselves. I wish I knew who the woman was."

"At this point there is no way to know. Of course if we poke around, we might just find out if someone is missing," I suggested.

"That won't be easy on a ship this large."

"We better meet the men in the atrium before they think we're missing in action."

I hauled myself off the bed and we left the room, making way for the elevator. Once we were on the lower level, I admired the elegant staircase that went up from two different sides, meeting at the top beneath an incandescent crystal chandelier that was centered over the marble floor below.

We moved past the staircase and into the atrium. The sound was deafening to me. We elbowed our way in and I couldn't see Andrew or Wilson anywhere, little alone a wedding party.

"Welcome aboard," said a man with a goatee, as he rocked to the dance club sound from a platform above dance floor.

This so wasn't my type of music and being in a packed crowd left much to be desired. I didn't have to say anything to Eleanor because she pulled me back out the door. She placed a finger into each of her ears.

"I think my ears are going to ring for a week," Eleanor said.

"You got that right," Mr. Wilson said from behind us on his scooter.

"Besides, they wouldn't let Wilson in there with that mechanical chair."

"It's discrimination, that is what it is," Wilson said.

"Of course it might have something to do with you running over some of the passengers' toes," Andrew said. "And would you believe the luck, it was the same couple from earlier."

"Not sure I'd call it luck," I said with a smile.

"How did it go when you visited the bridge?"

"Oh, you know, too complex for the most part. Eleanor nearly set off the alarm to evacuate the ship, though."

"We were planning to have dinner with the captain tomorrow," Eleanor said. "But we're not so sure now."

Andrew cocked a brow. "Oh, and why is that?"

I fidgeted as I asked, "Why would you ask me that?"

"I just thought there was a story behind it, that is all. Why did it take you girls so long to meet up with us here?"

"You're just full of questions, aren't you?"

Andrew gave me one of his, 'I know you've been up to no good' looks, and for the moment, I didn't want to tell him about the body we had found that turned up missing. "No. It's just that we bumped into Martha and she told us you two bailed earlier than the rest of them."

"A few ladies in the group didn't care to have us along, anyway."

"Still, that doesn't explain the lapse of time you've been gone."

"Are you sure you're not a cop, Andrew? You're certainly acting like one now."

"What can I say. I guess I know you too well, now. I can tell from the look on your face that you're hiding something. What is it?"

"Would you leave your wife alone? There's no sense in asking her. You'll find out eventually," Wilson said.

"That's what I'm worried about, the eventually. I'd rather know now what I'm up against."

"There's nothing going on," Eleanor said. "What are we going to do now, stand here all day talking about nothing, or should we find something else to do?"

"We could all take a nap," Wilson suggested. "I, for one, could use some sleep."

We all agreed and went upstairs. I winked at Eleanor, which meant I'd meet her in the hallway once the men went to sleep. It took longer until I knew Andrew was truly asleep before I tiptoed out of the room. Eleanor was in the hall, glancing at her watch when I appeared.

I waited to speak until we were halfway to the elevator, but Eleanor spoke first, saying, "It took you long enough."

"I know, and it took so long for him to go to sleep. I hate lying to him about that body we found."

"Are you sure that's how you want to handle that? It's a pretty big secret to keep from Andrew."

I knew she was right, but how could I tell him that once again we had planned to launch an investigation? "You know how he hates us investigating, and since the body disappeared, we can't say for certain that a crime has been committed."

"Yes, but we both know that we saw the body at the same time."

"I know, but we promised the captain to keep it under wraps, remember?"

"Yes, but how long do you expect to keep this a secret from Andrew? It's no way to begin a marriage."

Eleanor was lucky that Mr. Wilson didn't care if she ever kept anything from him when it came to crimes or our investigations. My Andrew was quite another matter. "I know, but right now we don't know what really happened to that body. If I hadn't seen it with my own two eyes, I'd have thought I imagined it."

"We've already established that, but what now?"

"Do you think that's standard policy to tell us not to tell any of the passengers what we saw?"

"Yes, especially when they don't believe a word we said."

"He'll change his tune when he gets the chance to look over the camera tapes. As you can tell, all the corridors have them."

"The tapes will also include our goings-on, if we plan to investigate."

We hustled into the elevator as a young couple staggered

their way out. They had obviously been doing some celebrating already. I pushed the button and went back down to the fourth deck this time, since that's where Martha was staying. "Perhaps Martha might be able to be our third pair of eyes and ears."

"You want Martha to help on our investigation?"

"Yes, why not?"

Eleanor gasped. "Because in the past, she hardly stayed on task. The first time she sees some young man she has a fancy for, she'll be long gone."

"Oh, I know that, dear. What I meant was, she could report back to us if she happened to overhear someone talking about a missing friend or wife. People just can't disappear in a puff of smoke on a cruise ship, you know."

"I know, but—"

"But what?" Eleanor asked, with hands on her ample hips now. "I'm sure many passengers look at a cruise as one big party."

"Fine, you'll see just how wrong you are."

"You mean you plan to prove me wrong, right?"

I suppressed a sigh, not wanting to let her know she hit that nail squarely on the head. When the elevator came to a stop, we strolled out and I wished we were wearing hats, since the sun was so bright, especially for Eleanor's fair skin.

"Perhaps we should go to a shop and buy a hat," I suggested. "I'd hate for you to get a nasty burn."

"I'll be fine. Don't you have sunscreen in that purse of yours?"

"Are you talking about the one I left upstairs?"

"Fine, it looks like you don't have money on you to buy a hat, anyway."

"Don't you have money on you, Eleanor?" Although she didn't have her purse, I stared at her ample bosom. "You know, like in your bra?"

"I'm not spending any money this soon. Besides, Mr. Wilson has us on a strict budget."

"Really? So the old man is controlling your purse strings. I never knew he had it in him."

"Well, there's no sense in having to wire home for money. I'm sure his granddaughter Millicent wouldn't appreciate that."

"Fine, let's get this investigation going already."

Eleanor led the way and we gazed out to sea for a time until some of the passengers came back from the atrium. Since most of them were older, I half suspected that they also wanted to get away from that loud music. One particular woman wearing white sailor-type pants and a white shirt was red-faced, laughing from where she was standing by the handrail.

I went over there, thinking about questioning her, until I overheard her say, "This is my eighth year on this cruise ship and it never gets old."

I turned in her direction now. "Eighth year, as in you go every year?"

"No, dear. I live here."

"That must cost a fortune," Eleanor blurted out.

"One hundred and sixty four thousand a year, to be exact, but what great fun. I can eat to my heart's content and dance every night. They have dance hosts, you know, for single ladies, or for when your husband doesn't like to dance. Mine never did."

"I'll have to keep that in mind," Eleanor said. "I sure like to shake a tail feather."

The woman's brown eyes lit up as she spoke and I admired her silver hair. "I don't think I could do that much cruising, but your life sure sounds interesting," I said politely.

"I'm eighty-six and quite able bodied, so why not? My late husband took me on many cruises and told me never to stop. The way I see it, I'm living the life he would want me to have."

"Don't you miss your family?"

"Yes, and I visit them whenever I get back to Miami." She began to whisper, "Actually, before I decided to live on a cruise ship, every time I came home to visit my family, they set me up to go out on another cruise. I knew right then and there that we both needed our space. Can't blame grown children who are so busy with their families."

"Sounds like you have the best of the arrangement." I laughed. "I'm Agnes and this is my friend, Eleanor."

"Nice to meet you girls. I'm Gloria Downey. Hopefully we can catch up later. I'm off to the casino now while most of the younger passengers are in the atrium. I, for one, don't care for that style of music, do you?"

"I don't mind it a little, but not at this volume," I said. "We're here looking for my daughter. We're actually on our honeymoon."

Gloria stared at Eleanor and then me, so I quickly added, "Our husbands are taking a nap."

"Don't they always. It's great to know people our age still get married." She dabbed at an invisible tear. "It makes me miss my late husband all the more." Gloria then turned on her heels, making way for the elevator.

"Where would we ever be able to find Martha?" Eleanor asked.

"Let's check down there," I pointed out. "She has to be here, somewhere."

"Living on a cruise ship? Can you imagine, Agnes?" Eleanor asked.

"No, I can't really. I don't think I need that much excitement in my life."

We continued down the deck until we passed Leotyne Williams, who was standing under the overhang and out of the sun.

"What are you doing here by yourself?" I asked.

"Wondering what you two are up to. Where you two are, trouble isn't far behind."

"H-How do you know about that? I mean, really?"

Leotyne winced an eye in our direction, her version of a suspicious look. "If you girls need any help, I brought my crystal ball."

That's all we needed, for Leotyne to tell us some clue that would not make a lick of sense to us, like always. I had better things to do then solve a riddle.

We smiled and excused ourselves without commenting about the crystal ball reference, and continued down the deck, practically running headlong into a worried-looking blonde. "Are you okay, dear?" I asked.

"I-I'm not sure where my friend is. I'm worried since she's not the type to wander off."

This was a big red flag, could it possibly be that her friend was the one we found dead? "I'm sure she must be around somewhere. It's a big ship."

"I-I know, you're right."

"What is your friend's name, in case I run across her?"

"Kacey Crawford. She has long brown hair and has a habit of twirling it in her fingers. We're here as part of a wedding party."

"You don't say. And how many other bridesmaids are there?"

"Actually, she is the maid of honor."

"I'm Agnes and I'd really like to help you find your friend. What's your name, dear?"

"Allie Cox. We're from Dayton, Ohio. Let me show you where the other girls are."

Allie led us to a nervous-looking group of young ladies. These were the same ones who were quite happy not that long ago when we were down on this deck, speaking to Martha. She then introduced us to a redhead, who she said was the bride, Liz Busch."

"Are you related to any of the former presidents?" I asked with interest.

"No, Busch like Busch beer. Or that's how my dad always told us to tell people." Liz laughed.

Liz proceeded to introduce us to the rest of the wedding party. Raven Garret was a vivacious African American in a hot, red bikini and Penny Hodge was a demure-looking woman in a white, one-piece swimsuit.

"This is Agnes, she wants to help us find our friend."

"Thank you. I just can't understand where she might be," Liz said.

"Is Kacey the type of girl that would take off with anyone?"

"Not at all. We agreed that we'd stay together."

"She did say that she wanted to change out of her swimsuit," Raven said. "She was getting as red as a lobster."

"And what deck are you on?"

"The fourth."

Hmm, she was on the fifth deck and not the fourth. "Was she speaking to anyone that you can remember?"

"We spoke to plenty of other passengers," Liz said. "But nobody struck me as odd, or someone that Kacey would meet up with. The ship has barely left port."

"Actually, I think we're further out than we might think. And there's nobody that would wish to harm her?" I immediately regretted asking that, as they stared wide-mouthed at me.

"What my friend meant was, she didn't have any problems at home that would cause her to become depressed enough to behave recklessly?" Eleanor asked.

Liz's eyes became quite round. "Oh, no. Nothing like that. Everyone loves Kacey."

"Do you happen to have a picture?" I asked.

Phones appeared in the hands of the bridal party and when I inspected the photos, it was hard to tell if that was the woman we'd seen before or not.

"We'll keep an eye out in case we see her and we'll be sure to tell her to contact you," I said.

"Thanks," Liz said. "I've been planning this wedding for a year and I want to see it go off without a hitch. My father wasn't too happy about the expense, but he didn't want me to be disappointed."

"I hope I can meet your fiancé," I said. "He's one lucky man."

Liz slipped on a pair of sunglasses. "Thanks, but hopefully we can find something to eat. My sugar is feeling low."

"Don't let us stop you," Eleanor said. "It's important not to let that sugar get too low."

Chapter Four

Liz led the wedding party away and up the deck.

"Earth to Agnes," Eleanor said, as she waved a hand right in front of my face.

"Would you stop doing that," I said, batting it away.

"I thought I lost you for a minute. What are you thinking?"

"I wish I knew if their missing friend might be the woman we found upstairs. Hard to tell by those pictures."

"Well, she has dark hair like the woman on our deck."

"I know, but that's hardly enough to go on. We'll just keep our ears open and ask Martha for help."

Just then, Martha came sashaying toward us. "What are you old birds doing on my deck again? I thought we agreed to stay on our own decks unless we were downstairs eating."

"And miss seeing your shining face, Martha? You look a little sunburned already."

"So does that friend of yours. You should know by now not to let Eleanor out in direct sunlight for too long."

"That's what I told her," Eleanor said and smirked.

"You so did not, but go ahead and blame me for everything like you have a wont to do."

"I was just kidding, Agnes. No need to get postal on me."

"If I was going—"

"Go on your own deck if you want to argue. I have a headache."

"That music too loud for you, Martha?" I asked. "That's a switch."

"I know. I'll admit that it was a little too much even for me."

She frowned. "So, why do I get the feeling you want something from me?"

"Because she does." Eleanor laughed. "It seems that we've found—"

"We aren't sure just yet, Eleanor." I softly elbowed her. "We just heard that wedding party on this deck has a missing matron of honor. Remember the group that was walking past the last time we were down here?"

Martha pushed a lounge chair underneath the overhang and out of the sun, sitting down and pulling lotion out of her bag. "Oh, the Busch party. I met them earlier. Which one is missing?"

"Kacey Crawford."

Martha pouted. "That's too bad. I hope the girl didn't get herself into any trouble." She glanced around and then whispered, "She had some clown hanging all over her until she told him to get lost."

That got my attention. "What did he look like?"

"Tall, dark, and creepy. I couldn't help but notice he seemed to be following that wedding party and then singled Kacey out."

"So, you met the wedding party?"

"Yes, but don't ask me for specifics, I wasn't paying that much attention. I couldn't even tell you where there were from."

"Okay, well keep your ears open and let us know if she shows up or if you see anything else out of the way down here."

Martha chuckled now. "You want me to take part in your investigation, don't you?"

"We're not on a case. I just couldn't help but overhear a woman is possibly missing is all."

"It doesn't bother me, but don't leave me out of the loop. What's really happening here, Mother?"

Eleanor and I sidled up to Martha and I whispered, "We sort of found a body that disappeared before the security personnel came up to check it out."

"And you didn't keep your eye on the deceased the entire time, like you usually do?"

"No, we couldn't."

"Someone on the stairwell came chasing after us and we hid in my room," Eleanor said.

Martha laughed. "Security must think that you're off your rockers."

"That and the captain. Hopefully he'll find something on the security tapes," I said.

"That seems unlikely. I mean, if I was someone who planned to commit a crime, I'd try to figure out a way to disable the cameras."

Martha sure mirrored my thoughts. "I'm not sure how I'll find out if the cameras were disabled or not."

"Check them out."

"Can you come with us?"

"No. I'm with the ladies of the Sunrise Side Lifelong Learning, don't forget, but I'll keep my ears open and if I hear about anymore missing passengers, I'll give you a call."

"Thanks, Martha. We should be able to handle checking out the cameras, I hope."

We walked away and passed the other ladies of the group that Martha was with. Pearl and Ruby gave us dirty looks, but I tried not to let it get to me.

"What's up with them?" Eleanor asked. "They're looking at us like we stole their men or something."

"Well, did you, Eleanor?"

"Did I what?"

"You know, you sort of had a habit of flirting with the husbands back in Tawas."

"Oh, great. I hope you're not referring to Frank Alton, again. That's old news. I never meant anything by it, really. I just enjoyed riling up Dorothy Alton."

I froze at the sight of a very familiar-looking couple coming off the elevator. "Do you see what I see, Eleanor?"

"Yes, it's Frank and Dorothy Alton, let's run for it, before—"

"Oh, Frank. Look who it is. Agnes and Eleanor."

Frank fiddled with his hearing aid now. "Wh-What did you say, Dorothy?"

She pointed a boney finger at us. "Look, Frank."

Frank looked up and just shook his head. "So, that's the reason you insisted that we go on this cruise."

"Well…" Dorothy began to pout, which always seemed to work with her husband. "I didn't want to be the only one on a cruise. Not trying to be mean here, but Frank, you're not much company with the way you keep that hearing aid turned down all the time."

"Nice to see you, Dorothy and Frank. Fancy meeting you here. You should catch up with Martha and the ladies from the Sunrise Side Lifelong Learning group. Why, Leotyne Williams is even here," I said.

Frank nudged Dorothy in the ribs. "You know, the group you got us kicked out of."

Dorothy turned on Frank. "I did not. I just made a few suggestions about how the group would be more fun."

"Denise is running the group just fine. You can't just demand changes be made just to suit you."

"Frank, I didn't mean to."

Eleanor and I snaked our way to the elevator while Dorothy and Frank were arguing, and by the time Dorothy noticed we were on the move, the elevator door had closed.

"That was close," I said. "I certainly didn't want to be in their company for the rest of the day."

Eleanor grinned now. "I told you how much of a pest Dorothy can be at times."

"I thought you were just saying that because you didn't get along with her."

"That's changed sometime ago. If we run into her again, how

about we give her something to do investigation-wise. That ought to keep them busy."

"She was helpful that one time, but let's just hope we can duck away from them for most of the trip, anyway. I don't mind having dinner with them on occasion, but we'll never get anything done with them hanging around."

When the elevator stopped at the fifth deck and the doors opened, Andrew and Mr. Wilson were standing there.

"I told you they didn't go far," Mr. Wilson whistled in his screechy voice.

"So, where did you two sneak of to?" Andrew asked. "I missed waking up to your beautiful face."

I made my way up the hall to our room while Eleanor went into the room she shared with Wilson. I used the facilities and dabbed on a bit of lipstick, retrieving sunscreen from my purse and applying it.

Andrew sat across from me the entire time with that questionable look on his face. "So, where were you really?"

"Did you know Frank and Dorothy Alton are here? We just saw them on the fourth deck, you know, the one Martha is on," I said, stalling.

"With that group from Tawas?"

"No. I think they came here solo."

"And you'll have me believe you were just visiting Martha on her deck?"

"Exactly. You can go down there and ask her if you like, but you should be able to trust me more than that."

"I should is right, but I just know you're up to something."

There was a knock on the door and Andrew answered it. Eleanor and Wilson ushered themselves in and he sat down. Mr. Wilson was using his walker now.

"What's going on?" Eleanor asked. "You both look like you were in the middle of something."

"We were. I don't suppose you'll fess up about what you two are up to?" Andrew asked.

Eleanor stared at me and shrugged. "Agnes, tell him."

"Eleanor!" I shouted. "You promised."

"I didn't exactly promise anything. It will make me feel bad keeping secrets from our new husbands."

Mr. Wilson just shook his head. "You shouldn't act shocked, Andrew. You should know how our gals are."

Andrew sighed. "Somehow, I think I need to take a seat, too," he said, as he plopped down on the bed. "Just tell me. I promise not to overreact."

I wish I could believe Andrew, but I knew him all too well. "Fine, Eleanor and I found a body on this deck at the end of the hall earlier."

"But when I checked to see if someone was on the stairs, I was sure someone was coming after us, so Agnes and I took shelter in our room. Luckily, he didn't catch up to us."

Andrew groaned. "Did you actually see someone on the stairs?"

"No, but I heard something that sounded like footsteps."

"And it never occurred to you that plenty of people use the stairs, that whoever it was might not have been coming after you at all?"

Eleanor's mouth formed a big O. "I didn't think about that. I guess I was a little nervous after we found the body that I panicked."

"And then?"

"That's when it gets strange," I said. "I called downstairs and security came up."

"And Captain Hamilton, don't forget, Agnes."

"Would you let me tell the story, Eleanor?"

"Sorry, I was just trying to help. No reason to get cross with me."

"I'm sorry, Eleanor. I didn't mean to. I'm just on edge now."

"Are you planning to tell me what happened when security came up?" Andrew asked.

"Well, it would seem that the body disappeared. Whoever killed the woman must have moved her body so it wouldn't be discovered."

"And who would do that?"

"How should I know, but we did hear two male voices out in the hallway and I thought they might be searching for us," I said. "One of them told the other to hurry, but I knew better than to look and see who they might have been. I was too scared to even look out the peep hole."

Andrew massaged his chin now. "You're certain that the woman was dead?"

"I think so. I took her pulse and didn't feel a heartbeat."

"That's hard to do sometimes. Since the body disappeared, you'll never know if the woman was really dead or not. What do you think the cause of death was?"

"She had one of those towels they put on the beds. I think she was strangled with it."

"And what did the captain have to say about the missing body?"

"I don't think he believes us."

"He thinks we're looney tunes from the way he looked at us," Eleanor added.

"I can't say I blame him. I'm having trouble swallowing the story myself. Did you recognize the woman?"

"No, but when we went down to Martha's deck, there was a wedding party that was missing the matron of honor, a Kacey Crawford."

"Like, they can't find her?"

"Yes, they showed us some pictures of her, but I can't say if it was her or not, but they both had dark hair."

Andrew stood and now massaged the back of his neck. "This is a big ship, I'm sure that woman will turn up, the one from the wedding party. How old were they?"

"Twenty something, but Martha told us that she saw a tall and dark creepy man following that bridal party and he tried to put the moves on Kacey."

Andrew laughed. "Why is everyone you're looking for dark and creepy, or goon-like?"

"Beats me, but I'd like to look into the matter."

"The captain will find out we're not making it up when he looks at the camera tapes," I said.

"We should check those out," Mr. Wilson said, struggling to his feet, until Eleanor rushed over there to help him up.

"We planned to, but you'll need to get your scooter back. I won't have you hurting yourself by walking too far with that walker of yours," Eleanor said.

I loved the way Eleanor fussed over her Wilson. It was kind of cute.

We left our room and waited until Mr. Wilson and Eleanor went into theirs. It wasn't long before Wilson came zooming out of the room with his scooter and we all locked up. First, we headed down to the end of the hall and Andrew searched where we told him we had found the body, and he opened the door to the stairwell and glanced inside.

"No clues so far," he said.

I spied something in the corner that shined. I went over there to check it out, and worked it loose. It was part of an earring. I held my hand out for Eleanor to see. "Look."

She pulled out her spectacles from her purse and balancing them on the bridge of her nose, she carefully inspected it. "Looks like a dolphin, but this could be anyone's."

"Exactly," Andrew said. "But keep it all the same, just in case."

I stared up to the camera overhead and took a look at where it was pointed. "This camera doesn't seem pointed in the direction where it would have picked up what happened in this corner," I said.

"It might even be a dead spot," Andrew said. "All cameras seem to have them."

"What about the men who were outside our room? It had to pick up that, and how about the one on the stairwell?"

Mr. Wilson looked up at the ceiling. "It's hard to tell if it's working properly unless someone can use a ladder to check it out." He paused, and then added, "I could take a look. I worked as an electrician."

"On a ladder?" I laughed. "Somehow, I don't see that as a good idea."

Wilson gave me a half-cockeyed look. "I happen to be quite capable of checking it out."

"Let's not try that, dear," Eleanor said. "I don't think you'd care to stay in the infirmary for the duration of the trip."

"Good point, sweet Eleanor. We're supposed to be on our honeymoon doing plenty of—"

"Sightseeing," I interjected. "See, it's agreed, no Mr. Wilson on a ladder."

"Well, don't look at me," Andrew said. "I wouldn't even know what to look for."

Mr. Wilson laughed, as he turned his scooter. "Lightweight."

"The captain acted like he was going to check the camera tapes," Eleanor said.

"Yes, but I'd like to know what is on them. If only there was a way—"

"You might want to find out if any other passengers are missing first and assess the situation before you try to get the footage on the tapes."

I smiled. "Oh, so now you're giving me permission to investigate?"

"You don't need my permission and you know it."

"Didn't you say we were going to find something to eat?"

"I hope so." Mr. Wilson whistled. "I'm famished. Naps do that to me."

Chapter Five

I trained my eyes on our way down to the main deck. No, I won't get used to the glass elevator anytime soon. Mr. Wilson was whistling to the tune coming through the speaker in the elevator. It was of a pleasant volume that didn't blast your ears like what they had going in the atrium. I'd ask around to find activities more our speed since there were plenty of senior-aged passengers.

The elevator opened and we followed Mr. Wilson, who maneuvered his scooter through the crowd. He made a clear path and we were soon in front of a gold door.

"Wow, this certainly is fancy," I said.

I really hadn't expected this ship to be so elaborate. We waited around ten more minutes, listening to the other passengers who stood close by, but so far nobody was talking about anyone missing.

"We'll starve before they open those doors," Mr. Wilson said.

I smiled. "You must be famished."

The doors finally were opened and a young lady dressed in a black skirt with a white ruffled shirt smiled. She took names and we were led inside. A chair was moved so Mr. Wilson could get his scooter close, but he bellowed, "I can sit on a chair, you know," Wilson sputtered. He proceeded to hop off the scooter and Andrew took ahold of his elbow, easing him into a chair. A hostess then moved his scooter to the far wall so that it was out of the way.

"Can we sit closer to the window?" I asked a server, as he greeted us.

"Sorry, everyone has assigned seats."

I fingered the linen tablecloth. "This place is too fancy for us," I said.

"What?" Eleanor said. "It's about time we eat at a fancy place."

I looked down at my blue-cropped pants and white shirt and said, "I think we're under-dressed."

"Don't worry about that. We loosen the dress code for the first day. We usually do expect our passengers to dress up to eat in here," the waiter said.

Our waiter took our order and we all ordered ice tea since it was this beverage was included with no extra cost. We ordered lobster tail and steak with julienne green beans.

Mr. Wilson rubbed his hands together. "I've always wanted to eat lobster, but never had the chance to try it. I bet it's better here since it's fresher."

"You can get fresh lobster at any Red Lobster back home," I said.

"Except that Tawas doesn't have a Red Lobster, you mean?"

"Saginaw isn't that far."

"Try an hour and half. My granddaughter has been too busy to take me all the way there since she started working at the Butler Mansion Bed and Breakfast."

"It must be nice having her live closer now."

"Yes, I just wish she'd take some time off. The girl needs to find herself a man."

That was what I've always thought about Millicent and although I tried very hard not to get too involved in her life, I did want to introduce her to a man she might like, but I was at a loss to find anyone who'd be worthy of her. Yes, I have gotten to care for the girl like she was my own daughter, or granddaughter.

Martha did a wave as she passed our table.

"I had hoped Martha would have at least stopped at our table to tell us if she heard anything about any missing passengers."

"She's too busy with her group," Eleanor said.

When Andrew raised a brow, I said, "We asked Martha to keep her ears open in case someone else has a missing friend or family member."

"We already told you about the missing matron of honor," Eleanor reminded him.

"And you expect Martha to be useful? Last I knew, she almost forgets her mind when she sees a handsome young man."

"I know, but I think this time it might be different."

"Fine, but don't say I didn't warn you."

I turned around and noticed that Martha's group was indeed sitting with the captain. I tried not to look in that direction. I wasn't about to alert the captain that I planned to investigate the missing body. He might not believe us, but I certainly knew what I saw wasn't a figment of my imagination.

Soup was set down and I tried it out, even though I couldn't exactly identify the green sprig that was in the broth. It must be a spice of some sort. I lifted the spoon, blowing on it slightly, before burying it in my mouth. It tasted quite pleasant, but that's when the back of my tongue felt strange. And then my ears began to itch, my stomach tightening and swelling.

"Oh, my. I don't feel so good. What is that soup?"

Eleanor stood up. "I don't know, should I go ask someone?"

I grabbed at my throat now. "Y-Yes," I choked out.

Eleanor began running in circles. "Someone help, please. My friend is having an attack."

The waiter rushed over, as did Martha. "What's going on, Mother?"

"I'm having trouble breathing right now and my ears itch like hell. What was in that soup, anyway?"

"Seaweed," the waiter said.

"We didn't order soup. I specifically put down that I'm allergic to seaweed. Are you trying to kill me?"

"Not at all. Do you have a EpiPen?"

"No!"

"We'll call the doctor right away."

"Are you okay, Agnes?" Andrew asked, with a worried look.

"I've never felt this bad before. If only this itching would stop. It's driving me crazy."

A man I presumed was a doctor followed the waiter to our table, carrying a medical bag.

He pulled out a stethoscope and pressed it against my chest as he checked my heart. Before I even knew what he was doing, he pulled out something from his bag, and stabbed me in the leg with it.

"What are you doing!" I shouted.

"You're having an allergic reaction."

"I know that. You could warn a body before you stab them, you know."

"Sorry, I believed that time was of the essence. I didn't want to see your face swell up like a balloon. I'm Dr. Gordon. Most everyone calls me Dr. Jerry." He smiled. "I think we need to get you to the infirmary post haste."

Andrew helped me walk to a wheelchair that was brought in. "Are you kidding me?" I said, as I sat in the chair.

"Don't you dare come with me, Andrew. You need to eat."

"I'm not about to leave your side."

"That's silly. Please, eat and pack me up a to-go bag."

Eleanor said, "Are you sure you want to go all alone? They already tried to kill you."

"I did not," the waiter said, with his hands on hips.

"He's right. It was just a little mix up. This is nothing like a shellfish allergy."

Andrew gave me a kiss and the doctor pushed me out of the dining room with the other passengers looking on like I was a car accident. I would have done the same thing if this had happened to someone else.

The infirmary was on the other side of the ship and when I was wheeled inside, there was another woman on another bed as I was helped on the one next to her. There was also a woman dressed in blue scrubs, who took my blood pressure and put an IV into my hand. "Is this necessary?"

"Yes," Dr. Jerry said. "After that IV bag, you can leave, but I'd feel better if we could monitor you for a few hours."

"It's just a seaweed allergy."

"I know, but I want to take precautions in case you go into shock."

"Shock! You're really being over dramatic, don't you think?"

"No, I can't afford another lawsuit. I mean, I want to make sure you're really doing okay before you go back to your room."

I pursed my lips now. Oh, sure he did. He just didn't want a lawsuit if I left and keeled over. The doctor and nurse stepped out into the other room and I glanced over to the young woman next to me, who wore a white bikini. I asked the blonde, "What did they get you in for?"

"Sunstroke." She smiled.

"I wouldn't expect that to happen so soon."

"I have a sun allergy, actually. It never takes long to bring on sunstroke."

"And you went on a cruise anyway?"

"Yes, I should have waited until later in the afternoon before I ventured near the handrail."

That made me think of a vampire, until she added, "To be truthful. I'm more a night owl and from Seattle. I'm used to the sun hiding behind the clouds."

"That makes perfect sense. So, who are you with on the ship?"

"My boyfriend Ricky."

"And where is Ricky, now?"

"Having dinner, most likely. I didn't want him to miss a meal on account of me. I'm Leah."

"Nice to meet you and I'm in the same circumstances, except that I had an allergic reaction to seaweed that found its way into my soup. I'm here on my honeymoon. I didn't want my husband Andrew to miss dinner, either. Besides, he's with my best friend Eleanor and her husband, Mr. Wilson. I'm Agnes."

Leah laughed. "Mr. Wilson like from Dennis the Menace?"

"Not exactly, but actually Mr. Wilson's real name is Mortimer and he hates that name and insists we call him Mr. Wilson."

"Can't say I blame him. Plenty of elderly, I mean senior-aged, people are used to being called by the proper Mrs. May or Mrs. Banner, at least that's so in my neighborhood, unless we know them personally."

She had a point. That was one of the reasons it didn't bother me to call Mr. Wilson by his preferred name. He didn't even want to reveal his true first name until we got our marriage licenses and Eleanor had insisted on knowing. We all agreed never to call him by his first name.

"I know just what you're saying." I gazed up at the IV bottle, realizing I'd be here for a while, so I asked Leah, "Have you heard about any missing passengers?"

"Missing?"

Since she obviously didn't react in an untruthful manner, I said, "I just heard the matron of honor of a wedding party was missing. Kacey Crawford."

"That's just terrible. You mean they're planning to get married on this cruise ship?"

"Far as I know."

"I'll certainly be on the lookout. She might have just wandered off. There are certainly plenty of hot men around here. If I weren't with Ricky, I'd have snuck off, too."

"That's just not safe these days. Wouldn't you be afraid leaving with a man you don't even know?"

"Not really. I do it all the time. I mean, before I met Ricky. He takes good care of me."

I wouldn't allow myself to shake my head now. I just couldn't understand the younger generation and their values, not to mention morals. Not that I was to judge. I just worried about them going home or to a room with men they didn't know.

"You have to be careful these days, especially on a ship. Crime is not limited to the mainland, you know."

"You sound just like my mother. She doesn't care that much for Ricky, either."

Since I was going nowhere soon, I asked, "Why is that? Does she have a good reason to feel that way?"

"He's a little older than me," she began. "He's fifty and I'm twenty-one."

I shouldn't be shocked, since plenty of older men preferred younger women to those their age. Luckily not all men were like that, like my Andrew. Lord knows that younger women certainly looked better without their clothes. I smiled to myself.

When I didn't say anything, she said, "You must be shocked."

"Not really. It's just how it goes sometime. You mentioned he was good to you, so it might not be all bad, but wouldn't you like a younger man who doesn't need medication to be with you?"

She laughed at that. "You're right about that, but it works out just fine. Ricky is a very seasoned traveler. We've traveled all over the world. This is my first cruise."

"I'm happy that you found a man you love. That should make your mother feel more at ease."

"Love? No, you don't understand. I'm just enjoying the travel aspect. I never said I'd stay with him forever. I'm hardly old enough to make that kind of commitment."

Now that made sense. "Be careful, is all I can say. Some men don't handle rejection that well."

I had a nice time chatting with Leah until a half hour later, a very tanned man with slicked back jet black hair came waltzing in. "Come along, Leah. You're being sprung."

My brow arched sharply at the man, who looked like a goon to me, but then yet another man with black hair also strode in. "Hello, Leah."

Leah's lower lip trembled now. "What are you do-doing here, Leo?"

"Didn't Ricky tell you that I was joining you two for the cruise? I even have the room across the hall from you."

The voices of those men had me rattled. What was it that set my nerves on edge? "What floor are you on, Leah?"

"That's none of your concern, dear lady," Ricky said.

"I know. It's just that I was hoping to have lunch with Leah tomorrow, perhaps. I've so enjoyed her company."

Leah's face lit up. "That would be great. Let's meet in the Hawaiian Lounge. I've been wanting to try it out. Ricky will be busy tomorrow morning on business."

"Oh, I thought you were on vacation?"

"I mix my business with my pleasure. Isn't that right, baby," Ricky said to Leah.

She shifted uncomfortably under his suggestive stare. "Yes, and a girl needs to spend a little alone time every once in a while, Ricky. Agnes has been so kind to me. She reminds me of my own grandmother."

Ricky rolled his eyes. "Fine, but you had better be back by dinner."

Leah pushed herself off her bed and walked with Ricky and the other man from the infirmary. I didn't like the looks of either of them and something told me that they were both up to no good. I couldn't wait until I could see Eleanor, so I could discuss my thoughts with her.

Chapter Six

I must have dozed off because when I opened my eyes, a smiling Andrew was sitting in a chair near my bed. "What time is it?" I asked him.

"Time to leave. You didn't even wake up when the nurse took out your IV. We thought we'd let you get some rest instead of waking you up."

Andrew really was a kind man and I thanked him. "You're so good to me, but I'd really like to get out of here. Where's Eleanor?"

"Having dinner."

"It's that late already?"

"Yes, you must have been tired."

"I didn't think so, but I suppose you're right." I rubbed my stomach now. "I could use something to eat, just not a big meal."

"I'm glad to hear that. You really need your strength because we're going dancing tonight."

"Dancing?"

"Sure, I wouldn't miss the chance to have you in my arms. I think I recall that you loved to dance."

"Yes, when I was forty." But it sure did sound like a great idea. Hopefully, it would give me the chance to find out if anyone else was missing.

Andrew hooked his arm through mine as we left the infirmary. When we made it to the deck, the sun had sunk lower to the west and it felt quite nice without having it glaring in my eyes. He led me into a smaller dining room and Eleanor waved us over.

"How are you, old girl?" Eleanor asked, with concern mirrored on her face.

"Fine," I said, as I sat down. I lifted the menu and ordered a fruit bowl and iced tea. Andrew raised a brow, but remained silent.

"I met the nicest woman in the infirmary," I said. "Leah. She's having lunch with us tomorrow, Eleanor, in the Hawaiian Lounge."

"Sounds good," Andrew said.

"Oh, no, you don't. It's only for us girls. I was hoping to get a facial at the spa tomorrow afterwards."

Andrew laughed. "Fine by me. I was planning to play golf. They let you knock the balls off the deck."

"What about you, Wilson. What are your plans?"

"I'll hang out with Andrew. I can't wait to see that clown try to hit a ball off the ship."

"I'll have you know that I used to play golf, about twenty years ago," Andrew admitted.

We all had a good laugh about that one. I enjoyed both the iced tea and the fruit, which tasted freshly cut. That's the problem of living back in Michigan, there's hardly any access to fresh fruit, other than when it was in season. Nothing beat a Michigan watermelon.

After dinner, we made our way over to the deck and Andrew took me into his arms as we watched the sun sink lower and lower. When I head the sounds of lively music, Andrew whisked me up to our room to change into dancing clothes. I opened my suitcase and inside was a map of the ship and a golden key. I sank onto my bed in shock. Where were my clothes, and why was there a map of the ship and a key?

Andrew turned and asked, "Aren't you getting dressed?"

"No. I mean, this isn't my suitcase. Our luggage must have gotten mixed up with someone else's."

"But you brought your suitcase on the ship with you."

"It must have gotten mixed up at the airport. My name tag wasn't on it, remember?"

"No. You must have forgotten to mention it." He then stared at the suitcase. "It sure doesn't seem that anyone would have a suitcase like yours."

My hands went to my hips. "Whatever do you mean?"

"Just that you don't see many paisley patterned suitcases."

"I've had this suitcase since the sixties."

"It looks like it."

"Well, I'm obviously not the only one to have one."

"Is there any identification inside?"

"Nope, but it's filled with men's clothing."

"Now that is odd. Perhaps we should turn in the bag to the main desk just in case someone might have lost it. You might even get yours returned."

"I don't think so. What makes you think that whoever owns this bag is on the same cruise as us?"

"Most of the passengers on that plane were headed to cruises," Andrew said. "That's what the stewardess told me when you were in the bathroom."

"I think we'll just hang onto this bag and turn it over to the airport if we don't find the owner. We could just leave a note at the main desk."

Andrew frowned. "Fine, but I guess dancing is off for tonight. We'll have to go shopping to get you more clothes. I can't very well drag you everywhere wearing one of those complimentary robes."

While Andrew was in the bathroom, I removed the map and key from the suitcase and hid it under the mattress. I didn't want to tell him about the items. It certainly was quite a coincidence that the suitcase contained a map of this very ship. I penned a note about the found suitcase to give to the front desk, including only my cell phone number and not my name. I felt I needed to be somewhat cautious since I didn't know who really owned this suitcase.

We passed Eleanor and Wilson's room silently. I had a million things to discuss with her, but we needed to do that privately.

The first store we went into downstairs was too fancy for my tastes and the prices were out of sight. "Let's try another store." I stared through a glass case that had Tiffany brand jewelry. Everything was sparkly and devoid of price tags. Just like my mother always said, *'if it doesn't have a price tag, it means you can't afford it.'*

"This store has only name brand clothing."

"A little too fancy for you?" Andrew asked with raised brow.

"Yes."

As Andrew escorted me from the store, he said, "You do know I'm not broke and I can afford name brand clothing."

"Perhaps, but that doesn't mean I have to have it. I'm into more casual clothing and possibly something a little fancier for dinner and dancing."

Two more stores later, I found what I was looking for, Capri pants and tunic shirts that were loose and flowy, perfect for covering up those extra pounds. Andrew bought me three sets and a white, one-piece bathing suit that there was no way I'd ever be caught out in public. I just don't think anyone wants someone my age flaunting around in swimwear, unless it's at night. I laughed to myself. I couldn't help it, but I was a little self-conscious about how my body looked. Oh, sure, I'd never let anyone know I felt that way. It was one of those things I didn't need to tell anyone.

Andrew also bought me a pair of sandals with seashells sewn into the straps along the front of the shoe. They were peach and aqua and I loved them. I also found a loose, yet form-fitting dressy shirt with sequins and matching black slacks for a fancier dinner.

With bags in hand, Andrew and I made our way toward the

elevator and I spotted Leah and Ricky arguing. I couldn't exactly hear what was being said. I just hoped everything was okay.

Once the elevator doors closed, Andrew asked. "Do you know them?"

"That couple? Yes. Leah was in the infirmary at the same time as me. We're having lunch together tomorrow. Do you think I should have asked her if she was okay?"

Andrew's brow arched. "Do you really think you need to get in the middle of another couple's argument? I'm sure it's fine. It didn't look like he was swinging at her."

"I guess you're right. It's just that she mentioned that she was with Ricky just for the travel opportunities. I hope he didn't find out that's all she's hanging around for."

"True, some men would be angry about that."

When we were back on our floor, Andrew grabbed my bottom and I giggled as we made our way inside. This was our honeymoon, after all.

☸ ☸ ☸

Bright and early the next morning, we were having breakfast in the Nook Room and admiring a beautiful view of the ocean. I had sunglasses on the table next to my silverware since my eyes were so sensitive to the sun, not too unlike Leah's sun allergy.

"So, where were you two off to last night?" Eleanor asked, looking quite presentable in a pink tee and white slacks.

"We went shopping. I picked up the wrong suitcase yesterday at the airport, apparently. We gave the desk a note in case someone reports their bag missing. Andrew insists whoever the bag belongs to is on this ship."

Andrew's brow furrowed and he just shook his head. "I don't think that's exactly how it was said, but fine. I wish there was at least identification inside, but I didn't see any when I looked in the bag and it had long-sleeved clothing inside."

"See, the person probably isn't even on the ship," I said.

"If I say that you might be right, will you let this drop?"

I bit into my orange slice instead of answering. We finished our breakfast of eggs and bacon and were back in search of Martha.

"I thought you didn't want to see Martha?" Andrew asked.

"Oh, I know, but I wanted to see how she's faring this morning. I bet she's hungover. I'd hate to miss a chance to rub it in. Why don't you and Wilson explore the ship?"

Wilson whirled his scooter around. "Sounds like a plan." As he zoomed off, Andrew raced after him, telling him to slow down.

We found Martha easy enough as she sat next to Leotyne Williams, who was wearing her standard long-black dress. She, of course, was sitting in a chair with an umbrella over it so that she was in complete shade. If anyone was a vampire, it was she.

Martha had her shades on and a glass of water with Lemon in it. The way she was massaging her forehead told me that she did indeed have a headache. "Out of my sun," Martha said.

I moved next to Leotyne and asked, "Did you find out if anyone was missing, like that matron of honor, Kacey?"

"She's not missing, as it turns out. She showed back up in the dance club last night," Martha said.

My shoulders slumped. "Are you sure?"

"Yup, go ask her yourself. They're hanging out in the pool area."

We excused ourselves and Eleanor whispered to me, "What's going on here? So she's not the one we found on the floor?" Eleanor paused. "Unless the woman you saw on the floor wasn't really dead, after all."

"No," I shook my head. "But I was certain." Or I thought I was. "But what about the men who were in the hallway, searching for us?"

"I'm not sure, but we might have blown it out of proportion."

"I'm going to speak with the captain later about this. Hopefully he can shed some light on the situation. If it's not this Kacey, it could very well be someone else."

"We could question the girl, at least. Perhaps if we see her firsthand, we'll be able to know if it was her or not."

I walked up the deck until we were in the pool area. The sound of laughter, coupled with the smell of coconut suntan lotion, was overpowering. I spotted the wedding party right away and we made our way over there. "Hello, so I hear Kacey showed back up and wasn't missing after all?"

Liz looked up. "That's about it."

"And where is Kacey, now?"

A brunette turned with a drink in hand. "I'm Kacey, what do you want?"

I swallowed hard now. It was the young woman we had seen on our deck, the one I thought was dead. "I was just glad to hear you were found."

"I wasn't lost. I met up with a man and went up to his room for a few drinks."

"Someone you just met?"

Kacey began to tap her foot. "You sound just like my friends, and I'll tell you the same thing, I can take care of myself."

"I heard there was a man following you yesterday."

"Which one, I've had quite a few men following us since we've been here. There's sort of a singles' atmosphere, in case you haven't noticed."

"Sorry, I didn't mean to bother you. So, no creepy looking men watching you girls?"

"That could describe a third of the men here," Liz said with a chuckle. "Don't worry, we'll keep an eye on Kacey here. I'm not about to delay the wedding on account of a missing matron of honor."

"I could take the job," Allie said.

"I won't have you girls competing for the title of matron of honor. I've known Kacey since high school."

"Sorry to have bothered you," I said. It was then that I noticed the frown on Kacey's face, but with her friends all here, I didn't see a way to speak with her privately. We were walking back to the elevator when Kacey caught up with us. "Are you doing down? I'm starving."

When the door shut, Kacey's eyes filled with tears. "I-I didn't want to tell the girls, but I can't exactly remember what happened yesterday and my neck is very sore, see?" She pulled down the collar of her shirt to show us a red mark on her neck.

"Oh, my. We found you on the floor of our deck with a towel around your neck. We thought you were dead."

Kacey shuddered. "When I woke up, I was locked in a room below decks. Luckily somebody let me out."

"Do you know whereabouts below decks?"

Her brow knitted and she shook her head, but then she said, "I remember hearing the roar of the engines. I must have been close to the engine room."

How would they have been able to hear her if she were near the engine room? "Did you pound on the door to be let out?"

"No, it was just opened. A man shook me awake and asked me what I was doing in the supply closet."

"So, he works for the ship?"

"Yes, he wore the blue pants and gray shirt that all the men who work in the engine room wear."

"How do you know what their uniform looks like?"

Kacey's face flushed. "Because he had a name tag that said engine room officer."

"Agnes is only trying to help," Eleanor explained. "I know these questions seem prying, but we want to find out who did this to you."

"Eleanor is right. I want to make sure what happened to you doesn't happen to anyone else." When Kacey relaxed her shoulders, I asked, "Do you remember the man's name who let you out of that room?"

Kacey smiled slightly. "I'm sorry, but I don't. I was still a little lightheaded. I couldn't even tell you what was in that room since it was dark. The only light streamed in from the hallway when that man let me out."

"How awful," Eleanor said.

I continued with my questions, not wanting to keep her too long. "Besides your neck, do you have any other injuries?"

"I'm not sure what you mean."

How would I ask her this delicately? "I mean, like if somebody slipped you a date rape drug."

She shook her head vehemently. "Oh, no. I think I'd feel sore if that happened."

"Do they remember seeing the man you left with?"

"No, I just told them I went to have a drink with a man so they wouldn't ask too many prying questions."

"So what do you remember exactly?"

"I'm sorry, but the last thing I remember yesterday was the cruise ship leaving port."

My face dropped at hearing that and before I was able to say anything more, Eleanor interjected with, "And what about a creepy man following you?"

Kacey's eyes widened. "Yes, there was a man doing that, but I thought I had lost him."

"Can you describe him?" I asked.

"He was tall and thin with dark hair. He smelled oily, too, if that helps."

It didn't really, but I said, "Thanks for sharing that with us and please be careful, Kacey."

"One more question though," Eleanor began. "Is there any reason anyone would want to kidnap you?"

"Does your family have money?" I asked next.

Kacey laughed now. "Oh, no. My family definitely doesn't have money. If it wasn't for Liz, I wouldn't even be here. She's footing the bill for my dress and the trip."

"That's kind of her."

"We've been friends since the sixth grade."

"It's great to have a friend like that. Reminds me of Agnes here. She once helped spring me from a nursing home, legally, of course."

I nodded with a chuckle in remembrance. "You better get back to your friends before they wonder where you are."

"And be careful, since you don't remember who might have led you astray. There are plenty of reasons young women need to worry these days," Eleanor reminded her.

We rode the elevator down and back up again and dropped off Kacey back on the deck where her friends were most likely anxiously awaiting her by now. Once Eleanor and I were alone again, she asked, "So, what do you make of that?"

I pushed the button to the main deck and said, "Seems like somebody slipped her something."

"Then why was she in the hallway with a towel around her neck?"

"I'm not sure, but if they hadn't slipped her something, then why wouldn't she remember? They might have slipped her something first and she tried to leave, so they choked her unconscious and she got away from them, finally collapsing on the floor where we found her."

"Until the men found her," Eleanor added. "If we had hung around a little longer, we could have helped her."

"Yes, or wound up in big trouble when those men found us."

Eleanor nodded. "I guess we'll never know now, but at least Kacey is back with her friends without too many injuries."

"I'm still shocked that she's not dead. I really need to brush up on my checking for a pulse skills."

Eleanor chuckled. "Oh, is that a skill you really want to brush up on?"

"Yes, it might come in handy before we call in a 9-1-1 that the person is actually dead the next time."

"There was certainly still a reason for an alert though, Agnes."

I led the way out of the elevator and added, "The only thing I don't understand is if they didn't intend to rape her, why lock her in a room downstairs?"

"I know, it doesn't make too much sense. Since her family doesn't have any money, it can't be a kidnapping."

"Might it be human trafficking? I wished she could remember the man who let her out of that room."

"We could check for clues near the engine room," Eleanor suggested.

Captain Hamilton blocked our path with a frown. "Could I speak with you ladies, privately?"

I almost said, 'Yes, but it seems there's no need to, now,' but instead swallowed the words and we followed him to hear what he had to say. We walked through a door and down a long corridor and into a room with computer screens being monitored by security personnel.

"Please have a seat ladies," Captain Hamilton said. He waited until we sat down before continuing, "I wanted to bring you ladies in here to assure you that we carefully monitor this ship with cameras. There's nothing that gets past us."

"Oh, so you checked the cameras in our hallway and you saw what happened to that woman we found?"

"Yes." He flipped on a tape that showed Kacey stumble up the hallway with a towel around her neck, collapsing on the floor where we had found her. "See, she's quite alone and alive. If you watch the next few frames, you'll see that you two happen along and check on her before running back to your cabin. Then the woman gets back up and takes the stairs down."

"What about the men that came into the hallway next?" I asked. "They might have been looking for the woman, even. She did appear intoxicated on the tape."

"I want to see the video of those men. I believe they were

responsible for giving that woman a date rape drug at the very least," Eleanor added.

As the tape rolled, two men did come into the hallway, but they were dressed in white uniforms and replaced a light bulb in the exit sign.

I jumped off my chair. "What? That can't be right?"

"One of them did look down the stairs for a second," Eleanor observed. "Are you certain those men are reputable?"

"They call in before they do maintenance checks and after. Believe me, it fits a very tight timeline. The woman you thought was dead was simply intoxicated, as you can see. I won't have you falsely accusing the staff unless you have solid proof that they're guilty of wrong doing."

"What about before that happened, like when the ship left port?"

"They were at a meeting during that time and didn't leave anymore than five minutes before this woman came out of that elevator. I hardly think they had time to give that woman something and if they had, you think they'd be doing a maintenance call?"

"He's right, Agnes. Besides, she had the towel around her neck when she came out of the elevator, not out of a room."

"Well, I'm sorry for calling you up there, Captain. I really thought the woman was dead, but I know now that's not the case since we found out the young woman returned to her friends today. We were just going to find you and let you know we were mistaken."

Captain Hamilton smiled. "I can't blame you for that and I'd want a passenger to call us if they think a crime has been committed or if someone is hurt or injured. I just wanted to prove to you both that I did check the tapes and took what you reported seriously."

"I can see that you have. I'm sorry for taking up your time."

"Actually, I was informed that you two do a little investigating back home. I'd sure like to hear about it at dinner tonight. I'd like you ladies and your husbands to join me at my table."

Eleanor beamed now. "Really? I've always wondered what it would be like to sit at the Captain's table."

"We're late to meet someone, Captain, so we'll see you at dinner. Please do show us the way out. You got me so confused with all the twists and turns on the way into this room."

"I'd be happy to."

Captain Hamilton led us out and back to the main deck and I stared at every doorway we passed to see if it led to the engine room, but no such luck. I guess I wasn't prepared for this twist.

Chapter Seven

Eleanor and I stared out to sea, watching the dolphins jumping nearby. I'm not used to being near the ocean or viewing marine life. If I was thirty years younger, I'd have loved to learn to dive, but at seventy-two I'm much more of a careful person, other than when Eleanor and I have unwittingly placed ourselves into danger on a case.

"So, what are you thinking, Agnes?"

"I don't know. Did you see anyone in that stairwell coming up after us?"

Eleanor squared her shoulders, her eyes wide now. "Well, I thought I had and we heard the voices of men in the hallway."

"So, them being glad nobody was up there and hoping not to be interrupted pertained to changing the light bulbs in the exit sign?" I asked, perplexed.

Eleanor looked down at the handrail. "It appears so. I just don't understand any of this."

"I made a mistake. I was sure she was dead."

"How was she able to climb down those stairs by herself?"

"Maybe someone else came along and took her down them." I sighed. "No, I just have to admit that I was wrong about everything and leave it at that."

"What about Kacey? Was she really held downstairs in a supply closet?"

"I'm not sure, but we're going to find out, or at least try to."

Eleanor searched my face. "But how, Agnes? How are we going to do that when we don't even know the name of the man who let Kacey out of that closet?"

"Well, we're invited to the captain's table."

Eleanor slapped her palms together and then rubbed them. "Ouch. You mean you're planning to do some fishing."

"Perhaps even request a tour of the engine room."

"I always knew you were brilliant, Agnes."

"Do you really mean that, Eleanor?"

She snorted. "Not really, but I sure wish I could have taken a picture of that look you just gave me when I said it."

"We should head over to the Hawaiian room and see if Leah is there yet. She sure seemed like she could use some female companionship even though she's young enough to be our granddaughter."

"Speak for yourself," Eleanor said.

We strolled along the deck, past pools and hot tubs filled with both younger and senior-aged passengers. Why, in one pool, they were even playing volleyball.

"That looks like fun," Eleanor remarked. "I have a nasty right serve."

"Perhaps later," I said.

A young lady dressed in the uniform of the ship held a clipboard, saying, "We can sign you up for later if you'd like."

"Sounds great. How about two," Eleanor said. "There will be three of us."

"Three?"

"We can hunt down Andrew by then."

"What if he's too busy to play volleyball?"

"Call him and ask. You're on your honeymoon, you know."

"You are?" The woman's face became animated.

"We both are, but my husband uses a walker, but we got him one of those scooters for the cruise," Eleanor said.

"He can use a walker in the pool if he wants. It happens all the time."

"Really?" I asked. I just couldn't imagine it. I gave Andrew a quick call and told him about our pool volleyball plans and then our invitation for dinner with the captain tonight. He agreed to meet us at two and I hung up the phone. "Sign us up, Agnes and Eleanor, plus two."

While she jotted down our names, Eleanor asked, "Where is the Hawaiian Lounge?'

"Just go in that sliding glass door and it's right there. You'll just love all the Hawaiian cuisine."

We thanked her and were off. A young man held open the door for us and we thanked him. We stopped in front of a host stand with fringed green fabric hanging off it.

"How many?" a woman asked.

Eleanor's eyes widened as she stared at the woman's huge gourds, or the ones covering the woman's lady parts.

"We're supposed to meet a young lady. I'm not sure if she's here yet. Her name is Leah, if that helps."

"I'm not sure, but you can take a look around."

I felt a tap on my shoulder and turned. It was Leah, wearing dark sunglasses. "Hello, there. I'm glad to see I'm not too late."

"Not at all. I think we're a little early. This is my friend, Eleanor."

While Eleanor and Leah said hello, I told the hostess we were ready to be seated. We followed the woman to a table, hypnotized by the sway of her grass skirt. Before we had the chance to sit down, someone raced over and put Hawaiian leis around each of our necks, and grass skirts around our waists. Eleanor giggled, swaying her hips widely.

"Be careful, dear. Don't want to throw out a hip," I suggested.

We sat down and Leah was all smiles. "I like Eleanor already."

"Most people do, unless she's after their man, but she's a married lady these days and has given up her evil ways," I said.

"Nothing wrong with that. I wonder sometimes if I shouldn't have listened to my mother and not come on this cruise."

Before I was able to ask her what she meant, the server came over and took our drink order, Eleanor and I ordered diet colas, but Leah ordered a pina colada. I tried unsuccessfully to mask my reaction because when the server left, Leah said, "It was a long night."

I couldn't help but notice that she still wore her sunglasses, but the server returned too soon to tell us the lunch selections. "Today, we have tender ribs with pineapple sauce, grilled chicken, or vegetables and shrimp stir fry."

"With what sides?" Eleanor asked.

"Rice, corn on the cob, and rolls."

Eleanor and I ordered the ribs and Leah ordered the vegetable stir-fry minus the shrimp, and once the server left, I asked. "Why are your sunglasses still on? It's not sunny in here."

Leah didn't answer, only interlaced her fingers.

"What did you mean that you should have listened to your mother, dear?" Eleanor asked.

"She didn't want Leah to—"

Eleanor slammed a palm down on the table and from the way Leah visibly jumped; it wasn't hard to guess why her glasses were still on.

"Sorry," Eleanor whispered. "I didn't mean to scare you. I was just going to tell Agnes that you could speak for yourself."

"That's okay. She was just trying to help. My mother doesn't really like Ricky, he's my boyfriend," she explained to Eleanor. "Anyway, last night Ricky's friend, Leo, showed up and I don't really care for him."

I took hold of Leah's hand. "Did this Leo hurt you, Leah?"

She pulled down her sunglasses just enough to show me her black eye. She quickly put them back up.

"I ought to give that man a piece of my mind," Eleanor hissed.

"Oh, no. Don't do that, Miss Eleanor. He's a real bad man. He killed his own mother."

I was shocked at that. "And Ricky allowed this man to hit you?"

"Ricky wasn't there when he did it, but when I told him what Leo did, he told me to keep my mouth shut. That he needed Leo for some kind of deal he had going."

"Did he force himself on you?" Eleanor asked somberly.

"He tried, but I gave him such a kick. I guess that's why he punched me. After that, Ricky came back to our room and Leo left." Leah clenched her hands into fists. "I wish I could have hurt him worse than I did."

"I'm sure you hurt him plenty. What kind of business does Ricky do and how is Leo a part of it?"

"I'm not sure, but I think Leo might be the muscle behind the operation."

"So, you really have no idea?"

"No, sorry, I don't."

"Did you call your mother this morning and ask her to wire you money from home?"

"I can't. I mean, I'll just hold out until we get back to Florida and then I'll slip away."

"But what about Leo? What if he tries to hurt you again?" I asked.

"Ricky promised me he'd make sure I would never be alone with Leo again."

"So that's it, then. That's how you want it handled?"

"Yes, I can't risk making Ricky angry. He has friends in all the stops in Mexico." Leah smiled now. "Looks like our food is here."

The server set the food down and I was less than happy that Leah was so resigned to stay on this cruise with Ricky, who had allowed Leo to abuse her. From the looks of Leo, I wondered if he was the type of person who might have given Kacey a date rape drug, and I wondered, too, if Ricky's business was human trafficking.

The ribs were heavenly and the atmosphere was great. If the view out of the glass windows wasn't of the pool area, I would have thought we were in Hawaii, for sure. Leah eased up and laughed, listening to Eleanor tell her stories about Mr. Wilson cooking his specialty tuna casserole.

"My mother isn't a very good cook," Leah said. "My dad did all the cooking when he was alive."

"Sounds like a smart woman to me," I said. "Sorry for your loss. Losing your father couldn't have been easy for you."

"Thanks, but he's been gone for a few years now."

"Still, it takes time to get over a loss like that."

Nothing about Leah's past told me that she was part of any scheme of Ricky's. She was an average student who chose to take a waitressing job after high school instead of attending a university, and that's where she met a number of wealthy men who took her on trips until she got bored and found another. "Ricky treated me the best of all of them," Leah said. "If it wasn't for those creepy friends of his."

"And it took you this long to figure that out?"

"Well, it wasn't until this cruise that one of them tried anything out of the way."

"I see. I still think you need to leave before this cruise is over."

Leah stood up and wiped her mouth, setting down a generous tip since the meal was paid for, besides her alcoholic drink. We walked outside and I smiled when I saw Andrew and Mr. Wilson. By the time I turned to introduce him to Leah, she was long gone!

So, there I stood with hands on hips as Andrew took that opportunity to come in for a hug. "I've missed you, Agnes. I'm tired after trying to keep up with Wilson."

I smiled up at him as I pulled away. "I can only imagine. Did you bring our swimsuits with you?"

"Sure did. I can't wait to see you in your swimsuit." Andrew winked.

I felt a little flutter in my chest now. I was quite happy to call Andrew my husband. He's one of the most debonair men of our age bracket that I know. He's a silver-haired fox in many ways and I've noticed he has even turned the heads of many of the younger women on this cruise. Of course he is seemingly unaware of this, which makes him a keeper, but I already knew that about my Andrew. Even when I knew him back in Saginaw, when he was married and I was working as his investigator, he never strayed on his wife. You just don't meet men like that anymore. I'm still counting my lucky stars that Andrew showed up in Tawas like he had, fresh from the loss of his wife. I lost my own husband Tom when I was forty and knew just how hard it was moving on with your life, but life does and should go on.

Andrew waved a hand in front of my face. "Did you hear me, Agnes?" He dangled my swimsuit from his fingers. "I brought your swimsuit. Why don't you and Eleanor get changed so we can show these people how us Michiganders play pool volleyball?"

"Can't say I ever played in a pool before," Mr. Wilson said. "Or if I'll even be able to."

"They told us you can use a walker in the pool. I hope they meant that they had one available for that purpose."

"A walker in a pool?" Andrew said. "This I have to see. Hurry up, ladies."

Eleanor giggled as Wilson tapped her backside and we slipped into a restroom and changed into our swimsuits. I frowned as I admired myself in the mirror, feeling less than satisfied with my reflection.

My brow raised when Eleanor joined me at the sink, her ample bosom displayed quite prominently in her pink one-piece. "I know," Eleanor said. "I was planning to keep my t-shirt on."

"Not sure if that will look better or worse, but sounds like a plan for me, too."

Eleanor's hands slipped to her hips. "And what exactly for?"

"To hide these rolls, for one."

Eleanor leaned back to get a better look. "I don't know what you're complaining about. Sure, you have a few rolls, but what person our age doesn't? Besides, I weigh much more than you, dear. If I had your shape, I'd be working it."

"On the dance floor?"

"Yup, that's exactly what I meant," Eleanor said sheepishly.

Eleanor and I joined the men and Andrew asked, "What's up with the t-shirt? I thought you looked great in that swimsuit."

"I-I just don't feel comfortable flaunting around in front of all these people in my swimsuit."

"Why not? That's what most of the passengers are wearing," Andrew pointed out. "And they are all shapes and sizes, I might add."

"And don't forget ages," Eleanor said. "I'm wearing my t-shirt because if I don't, something might pop out of it that I don't want everyone seeing."

"Th-That's good to know. She's saving it for me," Mr. Wilson said with a sly smile.

I didn't want to touch that comment and led the way to where the game was scheduled. The woman that stood there now with the clipboard was different than the last one. This one had her hair knotted at the back of her head and the name on her nametag said, Tasha Black, Cruise Director.

"You're the cruise director?" Eleanor asked.

"I sure am." The woman smiled.

"I wouldn't expect you to man this station."

"Jess is on break and I'm always on hand to help out wherever I'm needed. As a cruise director, I'd never ask anyone to do anything that I wouldn't."

"Sounds great. We're here to play pool volleyball at two, Agnes Barton and party."

Tasha ran a finger along the list and said, "Oh, I see you need a walker." She motioned over a man and told him to bring the walker and he raced away, returning with it not five minutes later. He then stripped off his uniform, much to the delight of the women nearby as their eyes widened, and smiles appeared from even the ones who hardly looked capable of smiling.

He put the walker in the pool and helped Mr. Wilson off his scooter and into the water. Wilson wore Bermuda shorts for the occasion and a t-shirt, with a baseball cap placed prominently on his head. Eleanor rustled in her bag, coming back with sunscreen that she rubbed on Wilson.

"Stop it, woman. I don't need any of that blasted stuff."

"But you'll burn, dear."

My only thought was that at least then he'd have some color besides gray, which is what his skin usually looked. "She's right, you know," I said.

"Perhaps you should stay out of this one," Andrew whispered.

I nodded and frowned, as I saw the Tawas group heading into the pool opposite Wilson and Eleanor. I loved that group, but Ruby and Pearl certainly were no fans of mine, but thankfully Lenore and Violet were there, too, and they were at least nice ladies. Andrew helped me into the pool and he pulled off his shirt, tossing it onto a nearby chair. Ruby and Pearl ogled my Andrew, but they weren't the only ones. I didn't let it bother me, though. He was mine now, and I must admit he had a shape worth looking at.

"Go ahead and serve first, Ruby," Eleanor said. "Hopefully you can play volleyball better than you can bowl," she taunted.

"Do you really hope she can?" I whispered to Eleanor.

"She can't hit the broad side of a—"

"Whoosh." The ball flew, winging Eleanor on the side of the face. She fell sideways and went down under the water, coming back up sputtering. "You old crow. Are you trying to kill me?"

I helped Eleanor back to her feet. "Hey, this is supposed to be a friendly game, not a blood bath."

"She's right," Violet said. "That wasn't very nice. You could have really hurt Eleanor with that fast ball of yours."

"Fastball, as in, she's known for it?"

"Her son has an in-ground pool and she's been practicing. Teach us to tease her for being a lousy player."

"Nobody says that anymore." Ruby nodded. "That's a point for us."

Luckily, Pearl served next and didn't get it over the net, and then it was Eleanor's turn. She tossed up the volleyball and slammed her fist into it. As it sailed over the net, it was hit by Violet, but when the ball was back on our side, Andrew spiked it to the other side. "Looks like that's a point for us this time."

Andrew served next and it sailed right over the net, too, but it was hit by Ruby, then Pearl, and then Lenore, before it made it back to our side. I hit it, but instead of it going over the net, the ball flopped to the pool with a splash.

"Good try," Andrew encouraged me.

It was now that I was reminded just how much I hated this game, which I doubly remembered when it was my turn to serve and I bruised my hand trying to get the ball to go over the net. Of course that never happened. I rubbed my sore hand and was about to call it quits when Mr. Wilson served, and the ball was dropped between Ruby and Pearl. The game went on for another five minutes before we were all exhausted enough to call it quits. The last thing any of us needed was to have a heart attack, since we were all over the age of seventy.

Once we were all out of the pool, we shook hands with our competitors and were given a free drink coupon by the activity director. Andrew and I walked arm and arm and sat on a bench near the handrail, and then Eleanor and Mr. Wilson joined us. Luckily we were quite alone, so I told Andrew how wrong we had been about the woman we had thought was dead, and how the men that came to that floor were only there to change a light bulb.

"That's certainly a change for you. Looks like you're out of a case."

"It wasn't a case, exactly, but I'm not done."

"I knew I was getting off too easy, please continue."

"Well, it seems that the surveillance tapes did record Kacey going down the stairwell by herself, but she told us the last thing she remembered was the ship leaving yesterday. How would that be possible?"

"She might have been given a drugged drink shortly after the ship left port."

"I suppose. She told us she woke up in a room below decks and that somebody let her out. I was wondering how she might have gotten there since on the tape she was by herself. I had assumed that she was locked in the room, but she told us she was woken up by somebody."

"So you're not sure how her story lines up," Andrew said.

"I believe her story," Eleanor said. "I think somebody planned to kidnap her for some reason, like human trafficking, perhaps."

"We're too far from Mexico for that, and even if we were near there, how would they get her off the ship?" Andrew said. "There has to be another reason somebody would want to kidnap her and lock her up."

"Some of the wedding party didn't seem too happy that she was matron of honor," Eleanor said.

"Are you suggesting that one of the bridesmaids would go to those lengths just to take their place as Matron of Honor if Kacey disappeared?"

"It wouldn't surprise me. Haven't you ever watched that Bridesmaids movie? Being in a wedding can be quite competitive."

"So that makes a few different scenarios, but I'm not sure we need to waste any time investigating any of them — if I don't want to at least substantiate her story, that is."

Andrew sighed. "Like how, exactly, question her friends?"

"Not at this point," I said. "But since we're invited to the captain's table tonight, we could fish a little. I'd love a tour of the engine room. That way we could poke around and see if we can find the place that Kacey claimed to be, or identify the man who helped her out."

I wanted to say so much more, but at this point, I just wasn't all that sure that the map of the ship and gold key had anything to do with Kacey's missing status yesterday. I should be relieved that she was safe now, but since we didn't know for sure if anyone had tried to do anything untoward to her, I just wasn't so willing to let this go.

"There's another matter on this ship that disturbs me," I began. "When I was in the infirmary yesterday, I met a nice young woman, Leah. Eleanor and I had lunch with her today and she had a bruise. I'm not sure what kind of business her boyfriend Ricky is into, but he certainly seems to allow his associates to abuse his girlfriend."

Andrew leaned back against the bench. "Just how many cases do you plan on focusing on while we're here?"

"I'm not on a case. I just hate to see any woman abused, was all I meant. I've seen her boyfriend and that man Leo. It wouldn't surprise me if they were the type who would slip a woman a drug in her drink. What if they were the ones responsible for doing that to Kacey?"

"I thought we were here on our honeymoon?" Andrew said, with a grim look on his face.

"We are. I'm sorry. I should learn to keep my big mouth shut."

Andrew took my hand in his. "I never asked you to. I just want the focus of this trip to be us spending some real quality time together. Tonight after dinner it's dancing."

"Sounds like a plan."

"I'm in," Eleanor added.

Mr. Wilson leaned on the handlebars of his scooter. "I can't dance in this thing."

"They have dance hosts that can dance with me, if you don't mind," Eleanor said.

"Just as long as I'm the one taking you home, sweetie. I don't want you missing out on the fun."

CHAPTER EIGHT

I put on the dressy black shirt with sequins and slacks with black ballerina flats that Andrew had presented to me when I was getting dressed. He was such a sweetheart, and just when I thought he'd never be able to surprise me, he seemed to know exactly what would not only look good with this outfit, but would be comfortable, too. I wore flats quite a bit, when sneakers weren't appropriate.

I admired Andrew, as he appeared out of the bathroom in a black suit, complete with jacket and red tie. This man I had married made my heart skip a beat every time he looked at me with those bedroom eyes of his. It wasn't a look he shot my way often, but it was enough for me to know that it held a promise of an amazing night to come.

When we went into the hall, Eleanor and Mr. Wilson were already there. Wilson was dressed in a suit and tie and fedora hat and it made me smile to see him so put together, when back home he wore the same green Dockers all the time. My heart actually swelled at seeing him this way. His cheeks had color in them until I raised a brow.

"It's a little blush. I didn't want anyone at the captain's table to think my husband was a ghost. Why, they might even try to bury him at sea," Eleanor said.

Eleanor positively glowed in a glittery blue shirt over white slacks, with flats on her feet. "You look beautiful, Eleanor," I told her. "I can't wait to sit at the captain's table. I just hope that Ruby and Pearl won't be there."

As we made way for the elevator, Eleanor said, "They ate with the captain last night. He needs to spread the wealth, you know."

"I know, which is why we need to make the most of tonight."

We waited longer than I thought we'd have to, but it was the dinner hour, after all. I stopped at the desk and asked the man attending the counter where we should go to find the captain's table. He picked up his phone and a man made his way toward us. "This way."

We followed the man past the dining room where we ate at last night and entered a room labeled the gold room, which had a sign that read: jacket and tie required. I raised a brow and Andrew gave me that knowing smile of his, like he had something up his sleeve or knew something that I didn't. At least he did his research, but the way I saw it, having dinner at the captain's table was a pretty big deal.

We passed under a huge golden chandelier and I felt, as much as saw, the warm glow radiated by the illuminating light that cascaded throughout the room. All of the tables were round, with the much larger of them in the front of the room, where two men dressed in all white uniforms cradled wine bottles in their hands. This table, like all the others, was covered with a white tablecloth and had golden silverware for the place settings, along with wine glasses, linen napkins, and coffee cups and saucers, the ceramic etched in gold.

It was then that I read the place cards and found ours nearest to where the captain would be sitting. Andrew held my chair out for me and I took my seat, graciously thanking him. Once Andrew and Eleanor were seated, one of the attendants removed a chair so that Wilson could get his scooter in closer.

"I think this is the fanciest place I've ever eaten at," Mr. Wilson said. "All that's missing is the dancing girl."

"That's after dinner in the atrium," one of the attendants said.

"Is that also where everyone can dance?" I asked.

"It sure is. We even have dance hosts, if your husbands aren't able to dance."

Mr. Wilson's head snapped up now. "You mean crippled, don't you?"

"I meant no offense. I just was passing information your way."

"Don't mind him. Post traumatic stress," I whispered.

"Not a problem. My grandfather has that, too. He's known to fly off the handle quite easily."

Mr. Wilson notably frowned now. "I'd love to meet that grandfather. I almost wonder if you're overblowing his situation."

"Let's have some peace and quiet now," I quickly interjected. "I don't want to be uninvited before we even have a chance to eat dinner with the captain."

"Not to worry. We'll fill your wine glasses," one of the men said, as he began pouring the white wine. "It shouldn't be too long before the captain makes his grand entrance, unless he's gotten himself into trouble."

That got my attention. "Oh, and what kind of trouble could the captain get into?"

The men glanced at each other. "He didn't mean anything by it," one of the men said.

"Oh, seems like he knew exactly what he meant."

"Who did?" Captain Hamilton asked, as he stood in front of his name card.

"Nothing. I was just wondering if you were the type of captain who was always late or early for dinner."

"Early, if I can help it. Seems like something always pops up that needs my attention."

"I can imagine that you've been kept quite busy. I wanted to thank you for inviting us to your table."

"It's quite an honor," Eleanor said. "I feel like I'm on an episode of the Love Boat, except that you're much more handsome and younger than that captain."

"So far I'm impressed with how well your staff attends to the passengers. Why, we even met the cruise director, who was helping out by covering for one of the staff so they could go on break," I said.

"We played pool volleyball," Eleanor added.

Captain Hamilton raised a brow. "I'll have to speak to her about that. This is her first cruise as director and she's supposed to delegate, not assume the positions of the staff unless we're having a shortage of help."

I frowned. "Oh, please don't censure her. I'd feel so bad for telling you that. It wasn't my intent to get her into trouble."

"She's not all that much in trouble. I was thinking a friendly reminded is called for, that's all."

I decided it best not to talk about this anymore, hoping that the captain would forget about speaking with Tasha about what we said. I gazed across the room then, as a loud and boisterous woman made quite an entrance, dressed in all lavender. It was Gloria Downey, the older lady who has spent the last six years on this ship. She pounded her cane on the floor until she had everyone's attention and only then did she walk over to the captain's table.

"Hello there, Captain Hamilton. I see you lost your stalker."

Is that what the waiter had meant by trouble? "Stalker?" I asked.

"Oh, yes. Captain Hamilton picks one up every cruise. This one is a vivacious woman of forty. I believe her name is Martha something or other."

Mr. Wilson about choked on his wine and Eleanor proceeded to rub him on the back. Surely it had to be another Martha. There had to be other people with that name besides my daughter.

"I hope she's not the same one who was with Eleanor and me that day we visited the bridge, Captain," I said.

"How did you know it's her? Oh, you're part of her group, aren't you, from Tawas, Michigan?"

"No, I mean, I'm not part of the group she's with. I'm on my honeymoon." I quickly introduced Andrew and Mr. Wilson to the captain and to Gloria. "But I do know her." I paused, thinking about how I should speak about my daughter, until I decided to just say it as it was. "She's my daughter."

Gloria laughed as she fell into a chair next to Mr. Wilson. "That's rich. She's quite a wild one."

"She's a free bird is all I can say. I'll speak to her about bothering you, Captain."

"It's fine. She's really not that much of a pest, but you know the imagination of some people."

I took that to mean that Gloria was gossip prone and made more of situations.

"Actually, my daughter rather enjoys the company of much younger men."

The captain leaned forward. "I guessed as much, since she barely kept eye contact with me when young men strolled past."

"Not even when she was speaking to you?" Eleanor asked with a laugh. "That Martha is something. Sometimes I think she was transported here from the sixties or seventies. She's very much the hippy type."

"Except that she's a little too old for that look," I reminded Eleanor. "But she's happy with the simpler things in life like living in my camper back home for one."

"Nothing wrong with that," Captain Hamilton said. "I think these days people are too hung up on how much money they can make and what possessions they own. I often wonder what it would be like to leave it all behind and lead a simpler life in the mountains, living off the land, even."

"Until a bear eats you?" Gloria said with distaste. "I see a few friends I'd rather dine with tonight."

I cocked a brow when she left so abruptly. "Wow, that was abrupt."

"Consider yourself lucky. That woman really makes my job difficult. I can't speak to anyone before she's telling everyone who will listen that they're stalking me, or that I'm acting inappropriately with a passenger. Even when she finally goes ashore in Florida, I think I'm finally rid of her, but sure enough she comes back."

"I think she told us that first day that whenever she goes home, her family sends her on another cruise."

"Wouldn't surprise me."

Denise Munson came over to the table and asked, "Are you okay, Eleanor? I heard that Ruby knocked you down with a volleyball?"

Eleanor rubbed the side of her face in remembrance, no doubt, and said, "She has a vicious serve, but it's all part of the game."

Denise began to tap her foot. "Nonsense. I won't have anyone on my group acting like that. I don't want to give you a bad impression of the Sunrise Side Lifelong Learning group. The members are all very nice, once you get to know them better. I'm afraid that it takes time for Ruby and Pearl to warm up to you, though. She'd like to apologize to you, if you'll let her."

"I'd be happy to hear what she has to say," Eleanor said.

Denise went off, returning with Ruby and Pearl, who had their arms linked like they were going to be sent to jail and would only do so together.

"Sorry, Eleanor," Ruby sneered. "I guess your big head got in the way of my serve."

Eleanor's face reddened. "Is that an apology, because it's the worst one I've ever heard."

"Ruby," Denise chastised her. "You agreed to apologize. What do you have against Eleanor, anyway?"

It was then that I noticed that Mr. Wilson hung his head. I put it together pretty fast after that, but I had to ask, "Yes, what do you have against Eleanor?"

I stared right at my friend for good measure and when she noticed me staring at her, she asked, "What?"

"Don't you what me. Somebody tell me what's going on here?"

Mr. Wilson looked up, then. "It's all my fault. I used to see Ruby, but she left town to take care of her mother. By the time she came home, it was too late."

"You cheated on Ruby with Eleanor?"

"No. I didn't know if Ruby was ever coming back to the Tawas area. She didn't either, until Eleanor and I had said our I dos."

"And you didn't speak to Ruby since she left town?"

"Not exactly. I did go to her mother's funeral, but that's it."

Eleanor jerked her chair away from Wilson now. "You did spend a long time in Saginaw. I should have known."

"I was visiting my granddaughter Millicent, remember? She came back to town with me."

"I just don't know what to believe, Mortimer."

"You promised to never say my first name."

"Well, you lied to me."

"No, I just didn't tell you about Ruby because it wasn't important. After we started dating, that was all that mattered to me. I fell in love with you, Eleanor, not Ruby."

Ruby balled up her hands into fists and marched away with Pearl chasing after her. "I'm so sorry," Denise said. "I had no idea there was any history between your husband Mortimer and Ruby."

"Quit calling me that. My name is Mr. Wilson," he shouted.

"Sorry," Denise apologized. "It might be better if we keep Eleanor and Ruby apart." She trailed after her club members and the captain smiled.

"Always drama at the captain's table."

"Oh?"

"Yes, we've had cheating wives and husbands. People who hated each other accidentally seated at my table at the same time.

It used to be amusing, but now it just gives me a headache." He laughed.

"I'm sorry about that," I said. "We certainly didn't expect Denise to drag them over here to apologize. After their actions today, I didn't see an apology happening."

"Volleyball upside the head, eh? You'll have to have extra wine tonight," the captain suggested.

We all laughed until two more couples joined us, Pat and Niles Busch, and Edward and Teresa Sloan. Before I had the chance to ask, they informed me that they were the parents of the bride and groom. Pat was a little bigger than her much thinner and muscular husband Niles, whereas Edward and Teresa were both thin and trim, and they also had an olive complexion, but I hardly associated the name Sloan as Italian or Greek.

"It's great to finally meet you. We've met Liz and her bridal party, but I have yet to meet the groom or groomsmen."

"That's because he's not on the ship yet. He'll be joining us in Cozumel. His groomsmen insisted on one last guy trip," Edward explained.

"Hopefully he won't get himself into any trouble."

"No, Brady has a good head on his shoulders. He's a medical student."

A sea of waiters came over and set down soup and returned to fill the wine glasses of the newcomers. The soup was very pleasant on the taste buds and devoid of seaweed this time, but I was almost afraid to eat it. I saw Leah and Ricky sitting not far away, with Leo and a few other men I hadn't seen before, but then this was a big ship. I was so intent at looking at them that Andrew cleared his throat. I then finished up my soup in time for the shrimp cocktail that I pushed to Andrew, who thanked me. He loved it much better than me. I was always so hesitant about eating it, but I sure did dig into the sea bass with steamed vegetables that were cooked perfectly. Not raw or too well done, just perfect. I tipped back more than a few glasses of wine and I asked the waiter for a glass of ice water with Lemon. I wanted to enjoy my night dancing with Andrew without being so tipsy that I'd miss out on all the fun like last night. I knew it was a mistake to drink before eating.

I was so stuffed I chose the green tea ice cream instead of the cheesecake the waiters offered. Eleanor indulged in it, though, since it was one of her favorites. My eyes met Leah's from across the room and I smiled. When she smiled slightly in return, Ricky turned and quickly scanned the room, searching to see whom she might have smiled at. That made me so mad. I knew a possessive man when I saw one and wondered if it was really Leo at all who had laid a hand on her.

Since dinner was not over yet, I asked the captain, "I'm very curious about how the ship works. Is it possible to tour the engine room?"

Captain Hamilton gave me a strange look. "That's an odd request, but if you're dead set on it, I'll allow it. In specified areas that are safe, of course."

"And is it below decks?"

"Of course. I'll have Tasha set you up a tour tomorrow morning."

That was easier than I thought — or was it? I had forgotten all about telling Eleanor about the map I found and that golden key, but I needed to do so and soon.

I pushed away from the table. "I need to use the restroom. Eleanor, come along, dear."

Eleanor stood and said, "She needs me to hold her purse."

"She can leave it here," Andrew said, giving me one of his, 'I know what you're up to' looks, but there's no way he knew.

We made it toward the bathroom and I checked inside to assure myself that it was indeed empty before I hung the temporarily closed sign outside.

Eleanor applied lipstick and asked, "Was that necessary?"

"Yes, I found a map of the ship and a golden key in that suitcase I have by mistake."

"Why didn't you say so before?"

"I don't know. I've just had so much on my mind and I'm trying to give Andrew the honeymoon he deserves and that doesn't mean knowing I'm holding something back from him."

"So, you didn't tell him about the map?"

"No, with that map it makes me wonder what somebody might have been about. What if they meant to do something desperate, like an act of terrorism?"

"If you actually have a key, it must go to something. We should find out what."

"That's what I was planning to do, but I wanted to see that engine room first. It's hard to read a blueprint of the ship, you know."

"So, you plan to bring the key with you?"

"Yes, and hopefully collaborate Kacey's story, if we can possibly find some evidence left behind in that room."

"Looks like that's not all you're worried about."

"Well, I'm thinking of watching those men who Leah is with. I still believe they might be responsible for what happened to Kacey."

"Just because they abused Leah doesn't mean they are traffickers, you know."

"It doesn't mean they aren't, either, Eleanor."

"How do you plan to watch them without Andrew noticing?"

"I bet they'll be going to the atrium for dancing later, too. I can keep an eye on them, or hopefully catch Leah alone."

Eleanor just shook her head. "Even on our honeymoon, we find trouble. I just don't get it."

I led the way back into the dining room and Andrew and Mr. Wilson were anxiously awaiting us. "Time to put your dancing shoes to use," Andrew said. "I've been looking forward to this all day."

"I hope you know that I'm not the best dancer."

"That's okay, I'm a good teacher."

I took Andrew's arm and we glided out of the dining room and into the main entranceway. The view of the huge chandelier overhead and the two sets of stairs going up on either side took my breath away every time I saw them. The atrium had a huge line and I speculated that it was about a ten-minute wait. Until Mr. Wilson whizzed through the crowd, clearing it for us. "Move aside, legally blind man driving," Wilson shrieked. He didn't have to tell them twice; people moved out of his way fast. We struggled to keep up, but luckily didn't lose him in the crowd.

This time instead of extra loud pop or rock tunes, there was an eighteen-piece string band with a sign that hung overhead that said, The Lennon Sisters.

"Do you see what I see, Eleanor?"

"I see it, but I don't believe it. The Lennon Sisters are here?"

"I don't think I've heard of them," said a young lady who stood near us.

"They were before your time, unless you ever watched the Lawrence Welk show with a grandparent."

"Is that even on anymore?" Eleanor asked me.

"Possibly it's played on some stations, not sure, but it should be. That show had the best performers on. My children certainly didn't love it when I watched it every week."

"You got that right," Martha said, as she joined us. "Every Saturday night right after Hee Haw. Gee, it's no wonder I turned out how I did."

"Don't you dare put that on me, Martha. You just turned out to be exactly who you are. Embrace it."

"Is it true you are stalking the captain?" Eleanor asked.

"No," Martha hissed. "Who told you that?"

"Gloria."

"That old bat is the snoopiest ever. She's been out to sea too long. It's warped her brain."

"That's not quite what the captain said, but he mentioned she was a gossip."

"Oh, yeah. I feel bad for him, besides that he has a great and exciting job."

"He seemed to admire the finer things in life. Mentioned that he'd almost want to leave it all behind to live off the land, even."

Martha laughed. "That's what they all say until they have to do it. I'm not exactly like that. I mean, I like having a roof over my head and food in my belly, but that doesn't mean I want to conform to society and get a job. I'd rather make my jewelry, which gives me enough money for the basics."

"Thanks to me for allowing you to live in my Winnebago, you mean."

"Oh, Mother," Martha said, and sauntered off.

"Martha is lost in la-la land, give it up," Andrew said. "I rather like her this way. I can't imagine her any other way."

"I know. That one time she was working as a realtor really didn't seem right, but as we all know, that never lasted."

The band began to play and Andrew pulled me out onto the floor, where we started our first waltz. I really loved to dance. I just wasn't all that good at picking up my feet, especially when the tempo increased. I stared near the door and saw Leah and Ricky, with the ever-present Leo, whose presence screamed 'creepy' to me. There was also a line of young men wearing suits and Eleanor was handing one a piece of paper, and then she was led onto the dance floor.

Eleanor held the man tighter than he was probably comfortable with, since he seemed to be shifting so he wouldn't have too much contact with her. I gave her a hard stare and she chilled out her behavior, being sure to stick her tongue out at me as she whirled past. I'd expect no less from Eleanor. It even brought a smile to my lips.

After a few whirls around the dance floor, I begged Andrew to let me rest. We found seats and I was so exhausted. Mr. Wilson kept his eye on Eleanor at all times. Who could blame him, after the way Eleanor acted during her first dance on the floor? She had since behaved herself, but was it a little too late for Wilson?

"Eleanor seems to be enjoying herself on the dance floor," I said.

"Humph," was all Wilson said. His eyes suddenly protruded and he raced forward with the scooter into the startled crowd, causing people to dive out of the way just in the nick of time, like synchronized swimming dancers.

With a screech he braked hard, and Andrew and I were on the move to see what the to-do was all about. Mr. Wilson was crawling off the scooter with a raised fist. "I saw you trip my wife, you jezebel," Wilson shouted at Ruby.

Eleanor limped to her husband and said, "It's okay. I'm sure she didn't mean to trip me up."

"I'm sure I did," Ruby sneered. "How dare you steal Mr. Wilson from me."

"That's water under the bridge, now. We're married and you were nowhere near Tawas the entire time Eleanor and I dated and were engaged," Wilson said. "We weren't together when I started dating Eleanor."

Ruby began to tap her foot. "Oh, and when did we break up, exactly? We never did, to my knowledge."

Andrew raced up and caught Mr. Wilson right before he was about to hit the floor, easing him down on the seat of the scooter.

"We dated, sure, but it's not like I called you my girl or anything," Mr. Wilson said. "And we hadn't spoken in over two years after you left town."

"That hardly seems like you had any claims on him, Ruby," I said. "You need to leave the happy couple alone."

Ruby's face screwed up now. "Or what?"

"Look, you're not doing yourself any favors here," Andrew began. "It sure seems like you would have moved on by now."

"I have. That was, until I found out he married Eleanor and they're on the same cruise on their honeymoon that I am on. It's like they're pouring salt into my old wounds."

I sighed. "Eleanor has yet to do anything to you that I've witnessed. Believe me, I know Eleanor well enough to know that she's all about rubbing salt into wounds if she has a mind to, but she's not like that anymore. I can't remember the last time she's even had a fist fight with anyone in Tawas and that's a serious improvement."

"She's right about that," Dorothy Alton said. "She used to like to flirt with my husband, Frank, to get under my skin, but not anymore. When she started dating Mr. Wilson, there was a real change in Eleanor and I think you need to leave her alone. Whatever was between you and Wilson was in the past."

"Thanks, Dorothy." Eleanor smiled. "We sure got into our scuffles in the past, but I'm happy to call you a friend these days."

"This ship is big enough for the two of you to never run into each other," I said.

"Huh? Every time I go out on the deck, I see one of you honeymooners and again at dinner or dancing. I'm getting sick of the sight of all of you."

Gasps split the air and Denise came forward with a disapproving frown on her face. "If it bothers you so much Ruby, perhaps you should stay in your cabin for the remainder of the trip. I'm really getting sick of your mean-spirited ways. There's not even a good reason behind it. I'm beginning to realize that you're a bitter woman. We came here to have fun, not deal with a whole lot of drama."

"Come along, Lucy," Pearl said. "Let's go back to our cabin."

Ruby pursed her lips and holding her head high, she strutted toward the door just as there was an announcement that the Lennon Sisters would be on stage in five minutes.

"I won't continue to apologize for Ruby, but when we get home, her membership will be revoked. I can't have someone like that ruining our trips," Denise said.

I watched as she left and couldn't understand why Ruby was treating Eleanor like this. I knew my friend enough to know that it wasn't on her part. She had never even mentioned Ruby that I knew of.

"Dorothy, come to our table for a drink," I said.

"I would, but Frank's in the casino and I'm afraid he might spend too much money. He loves to gamble, you see. It's hard to get him out of there once he goes in."

Andrew and Mr. Wilson volunteered to go with Dorothy to try and talk Frank out of the casino, which would leave Eleanor and me to investigate Ricky and Leo. Presently they had left the room, but I thought I heard them say they were going to the billiard room, where they would be able to smoke cigars.

Chapter Nine

I waited until the men had left with an agitated Dorothy before I said, "Come on, Eleanor. We need to do some investigating while the men are away."

"Aww, but the Lennon Sisters are just set to go on, see, they're about to announce it."

"Fine, but only for a few numbers and then we have to leave, agreed?"

Eleanor and I sat down and the lights went dim, spotlights hitting the stage as the sisters sang, '*May You Always.*'

Eleanor and I swayed our bodies to the mellow tune.

"They certainly don't make music like this anymore," Eleanor said.

I nodded my head in agreement. I wished now that Andrew was here so we could enjoy listening to the sisters together. I then glanced at the program and saw that they'd be here tomorrow night, too.

Applause split the air and the Lennon Sisters began the first verse of '*Easy to Remember.*' When I glanced around, I saw that even the younger passengers seemed to be enjoying listening to the music, the couples moving closer together. It was nice to see the appreciation of music from another time by all.

After the second song ended, I pulled Eleanor out of the atrium and she dragged her feet. "I don't see why we have to leave."

"Because we need to follow Ricky and Leo. They're supposed to be in the billiard room. The Lennon Sisters will be performing tomorrow night, too, according to the schedule on the table."

"That's right," Tasha said from behind us.

"Sorry, I didn't mean to get you into trouble with the captain by mentioning we met you outside when you were working one of the activities."

She rolled her eyes. "Captain Hamilton needs to relax a little. I'm good at delegating, but I don't do so by being uncaring or having the staff overwork, especially in the sunlight for extended periods of time."

"So he did speak to you about it already?"

"Yes, and he was told in a nice way to let me do my job, my way." She winked.

I really loved Tasha's spunk and she seemed very nice.

"Which way is the billiard room?"

"You know that's a man's domain, right?"

"I like to play pool, too. Plus, I heard you can even smoke cigars in there."

"Oh, I don't see you as a cigar smoker," Tasha said suspiciously. "But I'm not one to judge. My grandmother used to smoke a pipe until she became too sick. She passed away just last year and I can't smell tobacco without thinking of her."

"I'm so sorry for your loss," Eleanor said.

"What a great story," I added. "I bet she was a real character."

"You have that one right, but she always kept a pack of Camels close by in case company came over."

I laughed. "She sounds like my kind of woman. Could you please lead the way, now?"

"Oh, of course. And here I was blabbering on like a magpie."

"Don't you dare worry about that. We're just trying to sneak off while our men are busy trying to get someone out of the casino."

"I see. Well, come along, then."

Tasha walked down a hallway that led to the back as Eleanor and I followed. It made me feel like we were going into some kind of seedy club. Like she read my thoughts, Tasha said, "I don't know why, but they built the billiard room like it was a man cave, complete with a secret entrance." She pulled a loose stone and the door slid open. When we strode inside, all the men glanced up from whatever they were doing like we were infiltrators; perhaps we were. I did see Ricky and Leo playing pool, but they didn't give us much more than a passing glance before going back to their game. Either they didn't remember who I was, or didn't care all that much.

Eleanor and I took a seat in the extra large backed bar stools that swiveled. When the bartender came over, I had to smile. He had slicked-back black hair and a waxed mustache. He rubbed a hand over his ruffled white shirt as he asked, "What can I get you?"

"I'd love a bourbon." That sounded like a manly drink.

"No, I mean what type of cigar would you like?"

"Cuban," Eleanor said. "Unless you're too much of wimp asses around here to have them."

"They're illegal to have in the United States," said a man next to me.

"Oh, but I thought we were in international waters by now."

The bartender reached under the bar, coming back with a wooden box and opening it. "Cuban cigar as you requested, ma'am."

"We'd rather not be called ma'am, if you don't mind," Eleanor said. "We just want to be one of the boys tonight."

"Oh, do you, now? Like a couple?"

I smiled. "No, but plenty of people sure have said that. We're married to men and on our honeymoons."

"So why are you in here?"

"Because I wanted to smoke a cigar and drink bourbon."

"And play a game of pool," Eleanor said.

"Take a cigar and I'll light it for you," the bartender said. "If you can handle that, I'll get you the bourbon, but I wonder if you can even handle that."

I took a cigar, as did Eleanor. "Do you have a cutter for the end?" I asked. "It burns better that way." I knew this to be true since I'd actually smoked a cigar before. Okay, I was much younger and really drunk at the time, but I did remember a few useful tips.

The bartender cut the ends with a cutter and used a silver lighter to light them for us. I drew in nicely, since if I didn't it might not stay lit. I then held it between my index and middle fingers as I exhaled. My throat tickled a little, but I tried to hold back a cough since if I did that, I'd not only never get my bourbon, but might just be asked to leave. Eleanor puffed her cigar like a pro, blowing the smoke in the bartender's face. "Two bourbons coming up," he said.

"I'm impressed, little ladies," said a man with a cowboy hat who was sitting next to us. "I've never seen a woman smoke a cigar before."

"Oh, really? I'm sure there are plenty of women who might. We're not all Barbie dolls, you know."

"Never would say that. I have too much respect for women. If my mama ever heard me speak out of line to one, she's tan my hide but good."

Our bourbons were set down now, and I took a swallow of mine, breathing deeply as it burned a pathway down my throat.

"Women were put on the earth to serve us," Ricky said, as he joined us at the bar.

I pretty much wanted to give him a kick, but Eleanor was nearer to him.

"Is that right, now? In my experience, if you treat a woman bad, she won't stay around that long."

"I don't need them around that long, just long enough to keep my clients happy."

"Oh, and what business are you in?"

"Distribution. Hey, aren't you the woman who was with Leah in the infirmary?"

"Yes, and I was under the impression that Leah really likes you. Why, she even defied her mother just to be with you."

"That's good to know. It makes it easier that way."

"Her mother?" Leo said, joining his friend. "Is that what Leah told you? I suppose she forgot to mention that her mother and Ricky used to be involved. It's no wonder she doesn't want Leah around Ricky, since she's already been there herself, if you catch my drift." He laughed.

I didn't like what either of them was saying. "So, you dated Leah's mother and then her?"

"Yes, I'm not into older women anymore, no offense."

"You mean your own age?"

"Whatever. Did Leah say anything about me when you had lunch today?"

"Nope. She just had horrible circles under her eyes. I suspect you kept her up too late last night."

Ricky's eyes narrowed now. "That must be it. Nice speaking to you, what was your name again?"

Oh drat. That's the last thing I wanted to tell someone the likes of him, but I could see no other way out of it. "Agnes, and this is—"

"Maggie," Eleanor said.

Ricky and Leo left the billiard room now and I heard the man next to me say, "What a jerk. Give me ten minutes with the two of them and I'll teach them how to treat the fairer sex."

"Not worth it," I said. "Men like him aren't worth your time and they won't change, anyhow. It would teach him if his gal turns on him one day. You can only push somebody so far."

Eleanor and I put out our cigars, drinking the last of our bourbons before my cell rang. It was Andrew and I told him I'd meet him back in our room.

As we left the billiard room, Eleanor whined, "So that's it for the night?"

"Yes, I can barely make it to my room. I think that cigar made me feel sick."

"But we sure smoked them like a pro, eh, Agnes?"

"You have that right. I've smoked a few in my days and always when I was tipsy."

"Me, too. Also, I used to sneak my dad's cigars when I was just a kid, until I got caught and got a licking. He didn't spank me much, but when he did, I sure paid attention."

Once we were in the elevator, I felt even more lightheaded. "So, Ricky dated Leah's mother, too? Did she tell you that in the infirmary, Agnes?"

"No, but I'll certainly ask her at some point, but tomorrow, I'm more focused on checking out the engine room and figuring out just where that closet might have been where Kacey was found locked in."

"If she was locked in," Eleanor corrected me.

"I'm not ready to start jumping to conclusions about that and we shouldn't. We need to focus on facts and until we can prove that she's been deceptive, we need to keep our minds open."

"I didn't mean it that way, exactly."

I rubbed my forehead. "I meant no harm. I just feel so tipsy right now."

The elevator dinged on our floor and Eleanor took ahold of my arm and waited until I slipped into my room before she crossed the hall, entering her room. It was then that I began to yank off my clothes as Andrew came out of the bathroom.

"If I knew you were going to do that, I'd have called you sooner."

I ignored his question as I pulled on my nightgown. Once it moved into place, I asked, "So, how did it go with Frank?"

"Dorothy really is a worry wart. I had no problem getting Frank to leave the casino. Unless he just didn't want to do it for her?"

"Or, maybe he had his hearing aide turned down and he just didn't hear her."

"Probably a little of both."

I brushed my teeth and came out of the bathroom, slipping between the covers. The last thing I remembered was kissing Andrew goodnight and him asking why I tasted like a Cuban cigar.

Chapter Ten

I was enjoying my shower, until Andrew hopped in. I shrieked and hopped out. I just wasn't into this so early. As it was, my stomach was summersaulting.

"What's the matter? You used to love it when I did that."

"I don't remember ever saying I loved it. You just take it upon yourself to hop on in and disrupt my shower." I laughed then. "I'm not trying to be mean, but I'm just not feeling so good this morning."

"It might have been the cigar and bourbon I tasted on your breath."

"I brushed my teeth," I said in my defense.

"It has a way of sticking to your mouth like that. Where did you find a Cuban cigar, anyway?"

"In the billiard room. Eleanor and I were the only women in there. It's like a man cave. If we didn't smoke a cigar, I had a feeling that we'd have been asked to leave. The bartender wouldn't even give us our bourbons until we took a hit off the cigar."

"Why did you drink bourbon? You know you can't handle strong drinks."

"I wanted to fit in is why."

"And you went there, why?"

"Just checking it out, why?"

"And you weren't investigating?"

"No. I already told you there wasn't a missing person."

"What about your scenarios?"

"I think too much. All I want to do is tour the engine room today. Is it okay if just Eleanor and I go?"

"Sure, somebody has to keep a watch over Mr. Wilson. Especially since that Ruby acted the way she did last night. I swear yesterday she was following us, even."

"So you think Mr. Wilson has a stalker on his hands?"

"Yes. I also think you need to keep an eye on Eleanor, since Ruby tried to trip her up just last night."

"Good point. Enjoy your shower. I probably should get ready. I think I'll feel better after I have breakfast."

I walked back into the bedroom, closing the bathroom door behind me. That was close. If I had stayed in that shower too long, I'd never be able to put the map and key into my purse without him seeing it. I just wished I could let Andrew in on everything I did, but I didn't want to worry him. He might even put his foot down, since this was our honeymoon.

I pulled the map and key out from under the mattress and tucked them into my purse right before Andrew appeared next to me in the room.

"Are we getting dressed, or ... ?"

I set down my purse and said, "If only I felt a little better, Andrew."

"I understand. You do look a little green. Are you sure you'll be able to handle breakfast this morning?"

"I'm not sure, but if I was going to get sick I think I'd have done it already."

"Good point. I suppose we should get dressed unless nudist day is on the program for today."

I smiled, since I really would rather have just fallen into his arms right now. And also, I was feeling guilty about keeping the map and key from him, but I just knew he'd really insist I turn over the bag or alert the authorities. If I thought this ship or the passengers were in danger, I'd have contacted the captain at the very least. Since I had the map and they didn't, I felt safer about it.

Once we were dressed, we knocked on Eleanor and Wilson's door, with no response. I knocked a little harder and a young man poked his head out of the room that was next to theirs. "Would you stop that racket? It's only seven."

"I know. I didn't ask you to stay up all night and I can smell the alcohol all the way over here."

"I think that's you, dear," Andrew said.

"Oh, it's probably leaking out of my pours."

The man slammed his door and I shrugged. "Perhaps we ought to go down for breakfast without Eleanor and Wilson. They might be sleeping in today." Although that made no sense, since Eleanor always seemed to be up and about earlier than me more times than not.

I didn't even fidget when the glass elevator took us down. *Was it possible I was getting used to it?* When we arrived at the Breakfast Nook, there was quite a crowd and we were standing in the line outside the door when a face smeared against the glass from the inside. It was Eleanor who then waved us inside.

I moved to the front of the line, informing the hostess that our party was already inside, waiting for us.

"What are their names?"

"Eleanor and Mr. Wilson."

"I don't have anyone with that name down."

"I just saw her on the inside," I insisted.

"Hmm, we do have Cat Woman and Batman." She put up a hand and whispered, "They told us they were on the low down."

The hostess then cracked a smiled and said, "Come along this way."

We were led to Eleanor and Wilson's table and Andrew held out my chair. I asked the hostess before she left, "So, how would you remember everyone that come through here?"

"You have to give your names at the door. We like to keep track of the meals our passengers have. It doesn't take long to remember faces for me. I've always been like that. My mother used to say, *'Ginny, you never forget anything,'* which is right, but I try to downplay it."

"If that's true, has a Ricky come through here? He's with a younger woman, Leah. There's another man that's been with them, too. Leo?"

The hostesses' face stiffened. "Oh, yeah. I try not saying anything bad about the passengers so I should take my leave. If my boss catches wind of it, I'll be in big trouble."

"How about later, somewhere else?"

The hostess looked around and began to shuffle back. "On the second deck at six. I'll be waiting by the hot tub."

I felt a chill run through my bones just now, like somebody had just walked over my grave, but I couldn't explain it. "I wonder if Ginny knows more about Ricky and Leo then we do?"

"Could be. There was something about that look in her eyes that was unsettling," Eleanor said.

"I suppose we'll find out at six what she has to say."

Andrew raised a brow. "No case, eh?"

"Nope, just checking out a few things. I don't have the best impression of Ricky and we found out last night that he dated Leah's mother and now her. I'd sure love to ask her about that, but I don't want to cause her any problems with Ricky. She has a black eye."

"Black eye? Did she report it to the captain?"

"Probably not. She told us Leo tried something on her and when she refused his advance, he hit her, but I personally think either of them capable of abusing Leah."

"Stay away from them. If they are capable of hitting Leah, what would they do to you if you poke too close?"

"You're right. Today's activities revolve around taking a tour of the engine room."

"Good. Perhaps that will keep you out of trouble, then."

"Give it up, old man. There's no telling these two anything. They think they have it all figured out."

"I do not, Batman. I have plenty of questions that don't have answers. I'd like to know what happened to Kacey that time she disappeared. I'm not sure yet if it was real or staged. I just hoped to get some closure. She could very well have just passed out somewhere on the ship. I'm still not sure about her memory loss."

"Go ahead and check that out. It sounds safer," Andrew said.

"Be careful, anyway," Mr. Wilson said. "I left my Batmobile home."

I practically devoured my pancakes when we finally got around to ordering and our food arrived. I even slammed down an orange juice to replace any electrolytes I might have lost from the drinks last night. I wouldn't do that again. I didn't mind a glass of wine, but I draw the line with anything stronger, now for sure. It did give me some insight about Ricky and Leo. From the sound of it, Leah was here for more than his pleasure.

When we got up and headed to the door, I was shocked to see Ricky and Leo, who stared over at me. Had they heard what I had said about them? Now every nerve in my body was at attention. Eleanor looked over at them now, since I stopped dead in my tracks. She tried saving the day by giving them a friendly wave of her hand and I followed suit, forcing a smile on my face. Their faces softened then and they gave us a curt nod.

I kissed Andrew when we were back on the deck and he was once again chasing after Mr. Wilson on his scooter.

"I'm so excited," I said.

"To see the engine room?" Eleanor asked.

"No, that I'm investigating with Cat Woman. What are the odds?" I chuckled.

"We were in a funny mood this morning. Mr. Wilson always puts me in a good mood and never complains about me investigating."

"Andrew is just concerned is all."

"I wasn't trying to say anything, really. I-I just was making conversation, I guess."

We made way over to the bridge, where Captain Hamilton waved us over.

"This is officer Matterhorn. He's second in charge in the engine room."

"You can call me, Ben. I'm not much into formalities."

Ben was a larger man, but not in an overweight kind of way, he was just constructed of solid muscle. I imagined a body builder's body beneath his clothes.

"Nice to meet you. I'm Agnes and this is Eleanor."

"I hope you don't have anyone else on this tour," Eleanor said. "One of those ladies from that Tawas group has it out for me."

"I heard about that. She came to the captain's table last night, remember?"

Martha gave us a wave and came over. "What's going on here?" Martha asked.

"Nothing for you to concern yourself with, so go find yourself a man to stalk, I mean, flirt with."

Martha frowned now. "I'm no stalker, for the record." She gave the captain a forlorn look and slowly moved away. I instantly felt guilty, so I said, "Fine, you can come, but try not to interfere."

"You say that like you're up to something, Mother."

"Not at all. Just curious about how the ship works."

"Actually, that sounds like a drag. I was hoping I could talk the captain into strolling with me over to the casino. I get so mixed up."

"I'd be happy to, Martha, providing you keep your hands to home." He winked.

So he wasn't all that bothered by Martha, after all.

Before they moved away, I asked the captain, "Has there ever been any trouble onboard?"

Captain Hamilton's brows furrowed. "Not sure what you mean?"

"Crimes, plots to take over the ship. You know, the normal stuff."

He laughed now, as did Ben. "Sure, I'll admit there have been crimes, thefts, unfortunately, even a few rapes."

"And that one time the newlywed fell overboard, remember?" Ben said. "She had too much to drink at her reception and was quickly rescued."

"It's impossible to take over this ship," Hamilton said. "They'd have to take over the bridge and there's no way that would ever happen with Theo and Gunner at the helm."

"But they can't be there all of the time."

"Oh, you planning to hijack the ship?"

"Not at all. I just have a vivid imagination."

"Well, we better get going on the tour," Ben said. "We scaled down things so you could safely be in the engine room."

We followed Ben to a service elevator that went below decks, leaving Martha to fawn over the captain. We then followed Ben down a long, narrow hallway. This certainly wasn't what I had expected. There were doors along the passageway and I asked, "What is behind all these doors?"

"Sleeping compartments for the men who work in the engine room," he explained.

He pressed a code on a keypad just like all the other doors had. The door also had a lock that could be opened, which I assumed was in case the power went out since he didn't use a key. I'd have to try later to see if the golden key would open it.

He pulled out earmuffs, which resembled headphones that would mask loud noises and we were told to put them on, as did he.

When the door opened, the smell of oil and machinery wafted over to us, and even with the earmuffs on, I could still hear the hum of the machinery. I was amazed at the level of equipment inside and he painstaking explained the importance of each of the pumps, from the ones that transferred the oil to keep the ship balanced, to fresh water pumps and sprinkler pumps. It was really educational, but also so over our heads. Each of the beige pumps had a round turn handle, some of them red, others the same color as the pumps. What I found the most interesting among all the things that Ben pointed out was the engine telegraph. The bridge communicated with the engine room to change speeds via a telephone. It reminded me of the Titanic movie, when someone would manually move it from full to slow speed. There was even a steering gear down here that could take control if power in the bridge failed.

"Thanks," I shouted, so he could hear me.

He led us back outside the door and back into a different hallway. We handed him our ear protection.

"Thank you so much. I feel so much better now. So you could power and steer the ship from right down here?"

"Exactly. It's just a safeguard since I've never known the bridge to ever have failed equipment, but we could handle it if it did happen."

I smiled, looking up the long hallway. "I know this is off topic, but my niece Kacey lost her way and I think she passed out in a supply closet down here near the engine room, she said. Anyway, she told me that someone woke her up. The thing is, she lost a priceless heirloom she had with her and it hasn't been seen since."

"Is there anyone who might have helped her out?" Eleanor asked.

"When did you say?"

"She went missing the same day the ship left port and she was found the next day."

"I'll do some checking, but I'd be happy to let you check the supply rooms if you like, but I don't see how she could have wandered in one."

"Why not?"

"Because we keep the closets locked at all times."

So, she might not have made up the story, but how would I prove that she was ever down here?

"Thanks, but do you have cameras down here?"

"No, I mean we do, but they haven't been functional for the last year. The captain doesn't seem to be too worried about this area of the ship and I'd have to agree, since passengers never come down here."

"But couldn't they slip down here?"

"No, they'd have to have to a key to even get down here through that door," he pointed out.

"Oh? That makes sense."

Ben proceeded to open closet doors and I searched each of them, not seeing anything out of the way, until another young man came up the hallway and asked, "Is there a problem, Officer Matterhorn?"

"Willie, Agnes here says her niece was found in a supply closet the day after we left port. Do you know anything about that?"

Willie swallowed hard, his Adam's apple bouncing. "I-I know I should have reported it, but she seemed okay."

"Which room?" I asked. "She lost an heirloom she had with her when she went missing."

Willie led the way to a supply closet and unlocked it. He walked through it, opening another door with a key, too. "It was in here. I thought it very odd since both of these doors are always locked, as well as the door leading below decks."

When the light went on, I saw a woman's sandal laying on the floor. I picked it up. "This might just be Kacey's shoe, but no necklace."

"You need to report that to the captain, then," Ben said.

"I think I'll just check with Kacey again. She's good at forgetting where she puts things. I don't want to put out an alert if it's not really missing."

"How did she seem when you woke her up?" Eleanor asked.

"Disorientated. I escorted her back to her deck to make sure she got there okay. She told me to leave and I did, but I watched from the end of the hall to make sure she got in okay."

"Thanks, and nothing like this has ever happened before?"

"Not when it comes to missing passengers or ones getting lost down here."

"Thanks, Willie. You've been a great help."

"And thank you for the tour of the engine room, Ben," Eleanor said. "It was quite interesting."

Ben escorted us topside and when the door closed, I checked it to assure that it was indeed locked, which it was. I then took out the key I found in the suitcase, but it wouldn't even go in the lock.

I put the key back in my purse. "What does this key go to?" Eleanor asked.

"I'm not sure, but at least now we know Kacey had to have been locked in that room."

"By someone who had a key to get through both the locked door here and the supply closets downstairs," Eleanor said. "Didn't you notice, Agnes, that the same key was used to open all the doors?"

"You're right. Either whoever locked Kacey up works on this ship or has gotten access to the key that opens those doors."

"Might be a master key Ben was using. We should ask the captain about that. Doesn't seem like there should be too many master keys floating around. I bet they keep a log or something of who might have them."

"I love how you think, Eleanor."

We sauntered over toward the bridge, but stopped when we saw Ruby and Pearl shooting golf balls off the ship. Eleanor hid behind me, using me as a body block as we backed away slowly, then dodging in the opposite direction. Once we were on the elevator, I exhaled. "That was close. I bet if that Ruby saw you, she'd try to hit you upside the head with a golf ball."

"Why else do you think I was hiding behind you?"

"I can always count on you throwing me under the bus, Eleanor."

"That's what friends are for."

When we were back on our deck. I went with Eleanor's into her room, and Mr. Wilson was snoring loudly on the bed. "Looks like it's time for his morning nap," Eleanor said. We crept back out and I checked my room, but no Andrew.

Instead of wondering where that man of mine might be, I called Martha, asking if she was still with the captain, but she told me no. "So, do you know where the captain went after you scared him away?"

"No, but I know where your hubby is. He's playing blackjack with Frank Alton."

I hit the end button on my phone. "The captain is AWOL for the moment. I guess we'll have to catch up with him later. Right now, lets head to the casino, where Andrew is with Frank."

"Oh, boy," is all Eleanor could say, as we went back downstairs via the round glass tube, which is what I began to call the glass elevator.

We caught Tasha at the front desk and asked, "Have you seen that captain anywhere?"

"I see him all over the place, but not recently."

"Drat. I'd like to speak to him about something, but I suppose it can wait."

"Where's the casino?" Eleanor asked. "I'm feeling lucky."

Tasha rounded the counter and we followed her into the heart of the ship. When I heard the bells and whistles of slot machines, I thanked her and we continued on our own the rest of the way.

"If Dorothy finds out Frank is in here again, she's going to blow a gasket," Eleanor said.

"I can't believe that Andrew is encouraging his behavior."

"Perhaps we should find out just what they're doing here

before we jump to conclusions. If you listen to Dorothy talk, she'll claim that Frank has a gambling problem, but I don't know if that's true. I mean, sure I've seen him buying Mega Millions tickets, but who doesn't when the jackpot gets big," Eleanor said. "You know how easy it is for Dorothy to get bent out of shape when it comes to her husband."

"I've never known Andrew to gamble either."

"Oh, are you really sure you know everything there is to know about Andrew?"

I wasn't so sure now that she said it. "Good point."

We wound our way around the paperless slot machines and I saw Gloria pulling down the handle on one of them. You really don't need to do that anymore. Why, with one push of a button, the slot machine goes into action. The only issue these days is how many coins per play you need to use. I remember when three quarters was it. Now, you have to decide how many lines to play and how much you want to spend per turn. Too little hardly helps you make your money back, but too much and you can lose your money pretty quickly. It's always been my firm belief that you should never spend more than you can afford to lose. It doesn't hurt to approach it from a fun activity standpoint.

Eleanor's eyes grew big and she put a hand into her pocket, ready to put a coin in the machine before I stopped her. "These machines only take paper bills."

She then fished out a twenty and proceeded to put it into the machine.

"Don't stand there, Agnes. You'll bring me bad luck."

"Thanks. I'll look for Andrew, then, without you."

"All right then."

I just shook my head and Eleanor either didn't see me or really didn't care. It didn't bother me all that much since oftentimes, Eleanor slowed me down and it's not like I was here looking to question anyone. The captain was next on my list. I did still wonder about why somebody would lock Kacey up like that and hoped to find out real soon. At least nobody had turned up dead, yet. I bit my lower lip almost as soon as I said it, since that was never a good thing to even think about.

I heard a shriek across the room and moved in that direction. It was Frank Alton doing some kind of victory dance like you might see a football player do in the end zone after a touchdown. Why, the way he was twisting and turning, that man could throw out a hip. I wasn't about to say so, though, since he's never said anything to either Eleanor or me about some of the things we do. I must admit that we've had to run away from bad guys and gals before. Now, some might even wonder how I ran down a beach once, but all I can say is that when somebody chases you with a gun, you run.

Andrew was up and slapped Frank's back in congratulations. "Good play, man."

Frank took his seat. "It looks like lady luck is on my side." He frowned, now. "That is, if my wife stays in the spa long enough."

"Dorothy is in the spa, you say?" I asked.

"That's where you should be, Agnes," Andrew said. "How did the tour of the engine room go?"

"Engine room?" Franks said. "That doesn't sound like something a woman would be interested in."

"Probably not, but it was quite interesting. Did you know they can actually steer the ship from down there if the controls fail in the bridge?"

"That sounds like it might ruin one of your scenarios," Andrew said.

"How do you know what I was thinking?"

"I've known you long enough, Agnes. I know how you think. Isn't that why you wanted to go on that tour? Strange, I didn't see that listed as an activity."

"It's not. I guess the captain goes out of his way to accommodate his passengers."

The dealer gave me a hard stare and I clammed up, as the bets were put down on the table and he dealt the cards. Andrew asked for one card and Frank threw down his hand after asking for one, too. It didn't look like he was doing that well anymore.

"I don't get it," Frank said. "It's Agnes, she's bringing us bad luck."

"You might be right," Andrew said with a laugh. "From that look of hers, I think I'll be sleeping on the floor tonight."

"It reminds me of my honeymoon. Dorothy got angry about something that I didn't even remember doing."

"Sounds just like a woman." Andrew laughed again.

"I think I should go before I really make you sleep on the floor tonight," I said, waltzing away from the table.

I found Eleanor not long afterward and she did not look happy.

"That darn machine ate my twenty like it was candy. I don't think I'm cut out for this gambling thing."

"Good to know. We should get going now. I heard Dorothy is in the spa and I thought it might be good if we distracted her from coming into the casino, looking for her husband."

"That bad?"

"Actually, Frank seems to be on a winning streak, but I'm bad luck."

"Men!" Eleanor said with a snicker.

We left the casino behind and I glanced on the wall at the map of the ship and only then did I remember about the map that I had in my purse. "We should head back up to our room so we can take a peek at that map."

"Why don't we do that in the ladies room. I don't feel like going all the way back up there and coming back down to find the spa."

Chapter Eleven

We found the bathroom, and through the doors was a nice sitting room with a couch and television tuned to the Food Network. We eased ourselves down on the couch and I took out the map and unfolded it. We gazed at it like it was in Greek, since it was a blueprint really and not one we could read.

"There doesn't seem to be an x that marks the spot," Eleanor observed.

"I suppose that would be asking too much."

"Do you think there are terrorists on board?"

"I have no idea, but I think it's time I come clean to Andrew about finding the blueprints. I thought it was a map of sorts. I'm not sure how to proceed, now."

"And are you also planning to tell him about the key you found?"

I thought about that for a moment. "No, we'll keep that to ourselves for the time being."

"So, why tell him about the blueprints, then?"

"Because, dear Watson, I don't want it on my conscience if there is a plot related to this ship. We should go ahead and inform the captain about the map and the suitcase. He might have an idea how to proceed from there."

"That might be best. Andrew can hardly get mad at you if you tell the captain."

I folded up the blueprints and shoved them back into my purse. I know my plans were to check on Dorothy in the spa, but right now I wanted this blueprint thing off my back. I hated to be deceptive to Andrew, but he really gave me no other choice.

I went to the front desk again, but this time the cruise director wasn't in sight. Instead, Jess, the girl she had taken over for at the pool volleyball station just the other day, was working the counter.

"Could you page the captain? It's very important that we speak to him and soon."

"He's in the spa. It seems that there was an incident there."

"Where is the spa, exactly?"

She motioned for a young man, who took us to the spa. The door was wide open and a gurney was being hauled out, with Leah on the stretcher! I entered once they had wheeled Leah toward the infirmary, but only because I could hear the shrill shrieks of Dorothy Alton.

"Dorothy, are you okay?"

"No, I-I'm not. Th-There was this woman in a seaweed wrap and she was turning blue. I was so scared that I didn't know what to do, other than to call for help. I-I tried to do CPR, but it was so hard to do with the arthritis in my arms." Tears trickled down her face. "I tried the best I could, even gave the woman mouth to mouth. It certainly wasn't the highlight of my cruise, I'll tell you that."

I was at a loss for words. I really didn't know what to say to Dorothy.

"That's great," Eleanor began. "It's important to begin CPR right away."

Captain Hamilton came out of the back and walked in our direction. "What are you ladies doing here? I thought Ben was keeping you busy, I mean, showing you the engine room."

"We took our tour, if that's what you want to hear, and we found the room that Kacey Crawford was found in, just like we told you. It was locked, so whoever put her there had access to a key. Is there a master key?"

"What room, exactly?"

"Supply closet near the engine room."

"So, that's the reason you asked for a tour of the engine room?"

I didn't want to lie to the captain, so I said, "Yes, but Ben didn't know anything about it. We spoke to the man who let Kacey out of that room."

"And his name is?"

"Willie, but you can verify what I just said with Ben if you'd like, which brings me to my next question. How many people have a master key to open the door leading to below decks and to the supply closets? Whoever took Kacey down there had to have lured her there."

Captain Hamilton's face reddened. "Are you insinuating one of my staff is responsible here?"

"I can't say one way or the other. All I know is someone had a key."

Hamilton whipped a hand through his hair and said, "There are master keys, but nobody has them except for Ben and a few others. We have a sign-in sheet in the bridge with three keys."

"Why exactly is it that below decks doesn't have workable cameras?"

"I meant to fix that, but it's really not much of a threat. I can't see somebody trying to sabotage this ship."

"What do you think happened to Leah?" Eleanor asked. "She looked in a bad way when they hauled her out."

"Not sure. Dorothy alerted us, is all I can say. Her lips were blue, but she was administered CPR before we arrived. They had turned back to normal by the time we showed up. It appears that Dorothy saved Leah's life. We won't know her condition until later when Dr. Gordon assess her. We'll be arriving at Cozumel tomorrow and she'll be taken to shore if the doctor thinks he can't handle her condition."

"That boyfriend of hers might be worth speaking to about her condition. I believe that there's been some domestic abuse between them."

"She appeared to have a black eye just yesterday," Eleanor said.

"Thanks. I'll check him out for sure, but I can't say that he's been in here. Not too many men are, other than the metrosexuals. I'll check the cameras, too, but there are none back in the seaweed wrap room. We believe in giving women that come here their privacy."

"Do you have time to show us that key log, or…" I began.

"Sure. Whatever it will take to get you off my back."

Hamilton didn't act too shocked that we knew about the master keys, but he led the way to the bridge anyway. I figured that after we took a look at that log, we'd turn in the map that we had found.

The navigation officers, Theo and Gunner, were busy working at a computer panel while the other officers gave us a curious look. Captain Hamilton searched a drawer and asked, "Where is the master key sign-out sheet?"

Theo glanced up. "Officer Barber, didn't I see you with it last?"

"No, I mean I found it and was planning to put it back, but it has to be in there. I was sure I put it back in there."

"Perhaps you got distracted," I suggested. "If you trace back your movements, I bet you'll find it for sure."

The officer went to the drawer, tearing through it. He then stared and went back to the door and walked around, before he finally said, "I'm sorry. It appears I have misplaced it, captain."

"How about the master keys?" I asked.

"Without that master sheet, we'll never know who has them."

"Ben has one."

"He has his own."

Captain keyed open the panel and counted the master keys on the hooks. "There's a missing key. What is the meaning of this? You're the one who's responsible for signing out the keys."

"I know, but I can't remember signing out any keys to anyone since we left port."

Hamilton picked up a clipboard now. "Here's the sign-out sheet." He scanned the sheet and said, "It says you signed out the key, Barber."

"I did? Oh, yeah, I guess I forgot." He checked his pockets. "It's not in my pockets. I'll have to check in my quarters to see if it's there. Should I do that now, Captain?"

"No, just check when your shift is over. There was a passenger who apparently was missing and reportedly was locked in a supply closet below decks."

Officer Barber's eyes widened. "Oh, no. Is she okay?"

"Okay," I asked. "What makes you think it was a woman and not a man?"

"Well, I met that bridal party on board and they were very upset about their missing friend. I helped them search for her before my shift that day."

"I see. Nice of you to be of help, but let me know if that key was located. It worries me that a passenger was missing and locked in a closet. I'd hate to see that happen to another woman."

"I'll let you know," Captain Hamilton said. "So, if that's all, I have things that need my attention."

I stared over at Officer Barber, who was quite pale. Was it because he was on the hot seat with the captain, or for another reason?

"Could we speak in private? Like when you go to check on the cameras near the spa?" I asked.

Hamilton nodded. "Very well, follow me, then."

We followed Hamilton again down that narrow corridor, which led to the security room where they monitored the cameras. Once we were inside, we remained quiet as Hamilton requested the camera view of the spa and hallway leading to it. Buttons were punched until Leah was viewed on it, going into the spa. They changed up into the spa's lobby, where Dorothy was also on the tape, but the view was lost when they went into the back.

"There's nothing out of place with Leah," Hamilton said. "And no reason to speak to the boyfriend. Seems that you're barking up the wrong tree."

I sighed. "You might be right about that, but…" I reached into my bag and came back with the folded paper and handed it to him. "I picked up the wrong suitcase at the airport and this was inside, along with men's clothing."

Captain unfolded the paper. "I see. One of the engineers lost his bag and it must be his suitcase. He was bringing the blueprints for a few improvements that we planned to make on the ship. I'll follow you up to your room for the luggage."

I stared wide-eyed now. "I see. Well, I feel awfully silly now."

"Agnes has a vivid imagination. She thought someone had planned to disable the ship, or some other such plot. I guess we're too used to investigating crimes."

"No harm done."

"Perhaps this engineer has my bag, then. I'd sure love to get it back."

"Actually, he missed the ship. He'll be joining us in Cozumel tomorrow."

"Tell him to bring my suitcase, please. I had to buy more clothes for the cruise."

"I'm sure that was painful for you." Hamilton laughed.

"The price certainly was."

After we went upstairs and I handed the suitcase over to the captain, I plopped down on the bed next to Eleanor.

"Is there a reason you didn't hand over the key, or did you put it into the bag?"

"No, I think I'll just hand it over tomorrow when I meet the engineer, if there really is one. I'm not sure that Captain Hamilton is so innocent about the missing key, and now the blueprints.

Wouldn't an engineer keep them in some kind of metal cylinder?"

"That's why I love you Agnes. I love how you think. Yes, it certainly seems strange, indeed."

"So, what now?"

"Well, we need to find out if that key turns up or not. I still want to speak to the hostess at six. I want to hear what she has to say about Ricky and Leo. I still don't have them off my radar."

"Ugh, more work, then? You better not make me miss the Lennon Sisters tonight. You promised we could see them tonight."

"Don't worry, Eleanor. That is, if we can ever get Andrew out of the casino."

"I'm not about to let that get in my way. I better check on Mr. Wilson, though, and it seems we have missed lunch."

"There's no missing it. On a cruise you can always get a meal, remember?"

"It's no wonder Gloria has stayed on the ship so long. Kind of nice to never have to worry about cooking yourself a meal. There are plenty of times I just don't feel like cooking dinner."

Eleanor left and I walked over to the dresser that looked flush to the floor in the front, but there was a tiny gap in the back and I was able to wedge the key underneath it for safekeeping. You couldn't even see it raised even a little. Perhaps I should have turned that key over, but I just wasn't sure how much I should trust the captain now. Could he be the one involved with Kacey's disappearance?

CHAPTER TWELVE

I was just heading off the elevator when Andrew approached. "Hello there, beautiful," he said.

"Fancy meeting you here. Did you lose all our money?"

"No, I won, but not nearly as much as Frank. Dorothy will be a happy camper when she finds out."

I smiled. "That's great, but I'm heading to the infirmary to see how Leah's doing. She turned blue at the spa today. Dorothy saved her life from the sound of it, when she administered CPR."

"Wow, now that's awful and great at the same time. Run along and check on Leah, then. I'll be heading upstairs to relax before dinner."

"Don't forget that I have to meet up with the hostess at six, so I'll be late."

Eleanor came up from behind. "Where are you taking off to, Agnes?"

"The infirmary."

"Sounds great. Mr. Wilson wasn't in my room when I checked. I hope he isn't off somewhere getting into trouble," she fretted.

"I'm sure he's fine," Andrew said. "You really worry too much about him."

"I can't help it. He's my husband."

"I love the sound of that, but let's get to the infirmary."

Eleanor and I strolled toward the infirmary. On the way, we stopped to buy a hotdog and pop, which we inhaled since neither of us had had lunch. Despite my stomach still grumbling, we walked into the infirmary. Dr. Gordon greeted us and said, "Are you here for treatment?"

"Oh, no. We're just here to check on Leah."

"Is she doing okay?" Eleanor asked.

"I can't really tell you one way or the other, but I'll ask Leah if she's up for a visit."

Dr. Gordon disappeared into the back and returned with a smile on his face. "Go on back, but try not to get her too excited. I want her to rest."

I nodded as we walked into the back. Leah was laying on the bed, with the head raised slightly, and a cloth on her brow.

I sat next to Leah and took her hand, giving it a squeeze. "How are you, dear?"

Leah snapped open her eyes. "I'm doing fine, now, at least. It seems one of the medications and too much sun gave me a reaction. I forgot that I wasn't supposed to get direct sunlight when I took it."

"I see. I'm glad that's all it was."

"I was having trouble breathing. I heard a woman saved my life by giving me CPR right away."

"That's what we heard. Dorothy Alton to be exact. She's from the same town as us. I'm really shocked. I was surprised she even knew how to do CPR."

"I really owe her one."

"You don't owe me anything," Dorothy said from the doorway. "I hope I'm not disturbing you, dear. Nobody was in the other room, so I showed myself in."

"Of course, you're not disturbing me at all. Please come in."

Dorothy moved to the other side of the bed and checked the cloth, taking it and running it under cold water and placing it back on Leah's head. "There, that should be better."

"So, Ricky didn't have anything to do with what happened?"

"Well, he did remind me to take my medication and we spent time at the pool area, but I'd hardly call that an attempt on my life, if that's what you think." She laughed.

Who says it wasn't just that, but I smiled back at her. "I'm just glad you're okay, but can I ask you a question?"

"Sure."

"You said your mother wasn't very happy that you were dating Ricky, right?"

"Yes, that's right."

"But wasn't she dating Ricky at one time, too?"

Leah half sat up now, her eyes wide. "W-Who told you that?"

"Does it matter?"

"I suppose not, but Ricky wouldn't have told you. It must have been Leo. He's really trying to make my life difficult."

"You already told us that he tried to force himself on you, but why would he tell us something like that unless he's trying to make you look bad, or make us question why you'd be with Ricky when he used to date your mother."

"It's complicated, but suffice to say that my mother has a part in Ricky's business. When she found out I was seeing Ricky behind her back, she wasn't happy at all. She tried telling me all kinds of stories about how Ricky was only seeing me to satisfy his clients, but it's not that bad. I mean, I don't mind it most of the time. It's just Leo who I have a problem with."

I leaned back in my chair, at a loss for words.

"Not to worry, Leah," Eleanor said. "I'm sure you weren't aware of what Ricky expected from you."

"No, I wasn't, and by the time I found out, it was too late to turn back. We were in Milan at the time and the client was very hot." She laughed. "Hard to say no to that."

"So, it doesn't bother you that Ricky is prostituting you to his clients?" Dorothy asked was a huge frown.

"I guess I didn't see it that way, but they do spend money on me and I like that."

"Until Ricky gets tired of you and moves on to the next target."

Leah closed her eyes for a moment with a sigh. When she

opened them, she said, "I have been giving it some thought. I know that if I continue to stay with Ricky, it's only a matter of time before I'll be forced to submit to Leo and that's just not something I'm willing to do. I have enough money to leave him when we get back to Florida."

"Why not in Mexico?"

"I don't know anyone there. No, I'll wait it out."

It bothered me that she planned to continue to stay with Ricky, but there really wasn't anything I could do about it. "It's your decision, of course. I'm not judging you, Leah. I just want you to be safe and with Leo around, I'm just worried about you is all."

"I appreciate that, believe me. I should get some sleep. This medication really has me feeling tired."

I gave Leah's hand a good squeeze and Eleanor and I left. We weren't halfway down that hall when Dorothy shouted for us to wait up.

"So, is that it then, you're going to allow that boyfriend of hers to continue to have her sleep with his clients?"

"I don't see what else I can do. She's a grown woman and it's her decision, but I'm going to continue to keep an eye on those men. There was a missing passenger and I think they were responsible for detaining her, but I can't prove it yet."

"We're questioning somebody about Ricky and Leo later," Eleanor added.

"Well, somebody needs to. I'll try to come up with a way to keep that girl safe," Dorothy said, strolling off in the other direction.

"Dorothy sure seems to have taken a liking to Leah. Do you think that she'll really try to help her?"

"If Dorothy says it, it must be true. I don't think I've ever heard her actually try to help anyone before. I mean, she can be nice, but she isn't always, as you know."

"She might feel a bond with her since she gave Leah CPR. Leave it to Dorothy to save the day."

❈ ❈ ❈

With little more than that hot dog we had wolfed down, we met up with Ginny at the agreed-upon spot. She glanced around and disappeared into the shadows of the overhang.

"Thanks for meeting us," I said.

"Yes, well, I did want to speak with you about Ricky and Leo and some of the things I've noticed." She bit her lower lip and then said, "They give me the creeps and that's what the other girls say, too, but they haven't really done anything to me personally, just stared at me like they were undressing me with their eyes."

"Not exactly a crime," Eleanor said. "Plenty of men do that."

"True, I interrupted them one day when they were speaking to one of the other girls, though. Ricky was telling Roxanne that if she came to work with him, she's make way more money."

"And what happened then, did she take him up on his offer?"

"I practically yanked her back inside the Breakfast Nook. She was shaking pretty badly when we went back into the break room. She told me that after the way she'd seen Ricky treat Leah, it was more than enough reason to never go near Ricky. She then profusely thanked me for getting her away from him." She smiled. "But I've seen how those men look at the other passengers, or at least at the younger female ones. When I heard about that missing passenger, I was sure they were behind it, but when she showed up, I figured I must have been jumping to conclusions."

"I don't think you are. I thought that they were involved, too. At least one of the engine room personnel found her in that locked room."

"I hope nobody on the ship is helping him get access to the area of the ship where you wouldn't want a man the likes of Ricky going."

"Thanks for talking to us. Just alert the other girls to stay away from that man. I wish I could talk Leah into getting away, too."

"I know. Everyone on the ship knows that she's been sporting a black eye, but unless she tells the captain, there's not much anyone can do."

Eleanor and I went toward the dining room and Eleanor shuddered. "This is so frustrating. I just want to kick Ricky and Leo off this ship in the middle of the ocean."

"Now there, Eleanor. I know it makes you angry. It makes me angry, too, but we can't just take the law into our hands. We have to prove that Ricky is the one responsible for Kacey's disappearance."

"A girl can still have her fantasies."

We found Andrew and Mr. Wilson parked at the captain's table with Dorothy and Frank Alton. "We can sit here two nights in a row?" I asked the captain.

"You sure can when you're friends with Dorothy. I'm glad to know someone at this table is capable of giving me CPR if my heart stops."

"You're right about that. I'm so proud of you, Dorothy. I'm sure Frank is, too."

"She's stealing my sunshine. Here I was all happy about winning at blackjack and now nobody even cares."

"That's what you get," Dorothy said. "I told you to stay out of that casino."

"And that's exactly why I go there, to piss you off." Frank snickered.

We were joined at the table by the girls of the wedding party, the bride, Liz, Kacey, Allie, and Raven. Each of the girls was dressed in a matching dress in different colors of the rainbow. Kacey's face was pink and from the looks of the girls, they were all a little tipsy already.

"How are you enjoying the cruise, girls?" I asked.

"Great," Liz gushed. "I'm so looking forward to seeing Brady." She pouted. "I've never been separated from him this long before.

I hope he hasn't gotten into any trouble in Cozumel. You know men get a little carried away at a bachelor party."

"He went there just for a bachelor party?"

"Oh, no. His groomsmen insisted that he take one last guy trip with them."

"I'm sure it's fine," Kacey said. "Brady loves you and you're going to be married in just a few days."

Allie shook her head sadly. "Are you sure you're ready to get married, Liz? You're only twenty-three."

"Of course, Allie," Liz said. "Brady is going to be a surgeon one day."

Eleanor scoffed at that. "I'm sure that can't be the only reason. You must love him, right?"

"I do, I mean we've known each other since high school. It's only natural for us to take the next step."

"That's no way to talk, young lady," Eleanor said. "You get married because you're in love, not for any other reason. I made that mistake with my first husband and it sadly ended with him straying. Not an experience I'd wish on anyone else, I can tell you that."

"So, you were high school sweethearts?" I asked Liz.

"Yes, until he went away to school."

"So, how did you wind up engaged if he went away to school?"

"I marched up to that school and told Brady that I wasn't letting him go."

"Like a stalker, you mean," Eleanor said. "Got ya."

"She's no stalker," Liz's mother Pat said, as she joined her daughter. "If you want a man, you need to grab the bull by the horns and show him how much you care. That's what I did with Liz's father, Niles. He had a mind to chase after a girl on the next block. We were also high school sweethearts," Pat explained. "It only took me opening up the car door and almost catching them at the act before Niles opened his eyes. Of course I didn't speak to him for a few days after that, but in those two days, he sent flowers and candy, even bought me a puppy. In the end I finally did speak to him again and when I did, he went down on one knee and proposed."

"How old were you at the time?" Eleanor asked.

"Seventeen. My parents weren't too happy at first, but they knew his father owned a hardware store and that he would be partial owner after graduation. Busch's Tools." She fingered Liz's hair. "It was the longest year of my life. I wasn't about to marry a man unless he had something going for him."

Eleanor's eyes narrowed. "So, love didn't come into the equation, just money?"

"Don't get me wrong. I loved Niles back then as much as any girl would love her high school sweetheart, but I wasn't about to be a struggling newlywed. I was very young back then."

Eleanor excused herself and trounced away toward the bathroom in a huff. These Busch women seemed to be of a like mind and I just couldn't believe that they were that crude about marriage. Why, when I married my Tom, I was deeply in love and we could barely wait until we said our' I do's' before we were all over each other. I laughed at the memory.

Andrew nudged me. "Are you okay?"

"Yes, just happy that I married you for love and no other reason. I have my own social security."

Everyone at the table laughed, except for Liz and her mother, but I didn't give a hoot what they thought. I know it's not good to judge, but both of them certainly gave me cause to. I excused myself now, since all they were focused on was how much they had sunk into their wedding. Hardly a topic for dinner conversation.

When I strolled into the bathroom, Eleanor was washing her hands.

"Can you believe those women back there? I didn't mean I didn't love my ex-husband, but I sure did see the signs that he was a no-good cheater well before the wedding. I caught him in a compromising situation with Barbara Jean and she was my matron of honor!"

"I'm sorry you had to go through that, Eleanor, but at least you did much better with Mr. Wilson."

Eleanor smiled. "I certainly did, we are both very lucky to have men like ours. I just hated how love seemed out of the equation with Liz and her mother. The apple certainly doesn't fall far from the tree. It would teach her if Brady never boarded the ship."

"Now, Eleanor, that's no way to talk. It's not really our business. Don't make any waves."

"Fine, but I so want to tell Liz's fiancé what she's all about."

"He might already know. I also hope she knows medical students struggle enough in school and it will be many years before he'll be making any big amount of money."

"Good to know. I feel much better knowing that. We better head back. I'm starved."

By the time we came back, Caesar salads were at our places and half-full glasses of wine. I tried not to take a sip, since I hadn't eaten all that much today, but I couldn't help it. I then began eating my salad, but frowned.

"What's that matter with your salad?" Captain Hamilton asked.

"Nothing besides that it needs more dressing."

"It's thicker than most dressing, but we'll get you more."

Hamilton waved a waiter over and told him to bring more dressing. The waiter left, returning with it in record speed. I took the small bowl and thanked him.

"I must say that I'm impressed with the staff on this ship."

"Thanks, Agnes. We only hire the best. I kind of stole quite a few from the Princess lines. Let's just say I watch my back when I go ashore in Mexico, not that I do that often. Only if a passenger hasn't returned."

"Does that happen often?" Eleanor asked.

"Not at all. Many of the passengers don't even go ashore."

"Can't blame them," Eleanor said. "Just think, no big crowds and you have more time in the pool or Jacuzzi."

"That's how some passengers do feel."

"I'm going ashore for sure," Allie said. "I'd like to go shopping."

"You won't have time," Liz said. "Mom wants us to do our rehearsal tomorrow."

"But you have to wait until Brady shows up, so why not?"

"Allie's right," Raven said. "We deserve time to do a little shopping."

"You're here for my wedding, not for your shopping trip," Liz said.

"I paid for my own ticket and I'm going shopping and that's it. I'm not about to let some bossy white girl order me around."

I hadn't paid all the much attention the other day, but I realized one of the bridesmaids was missing. "Where is Penny? I haven't seen her in a while," I said.

"She's been seasick," Kacey said. "She's planning to get acupuncture to cure it tonight."

"Does that actually work?" Eleanor asked.

"It really works," Captain Hamilton said. "Don't be shocked. I told you we only employ the most experienced of staff. We have a girl from China who was trained to do acupuncture by her grandmother when she was only a child. I've had her work on me for muscle cramps before. I've never had one since."

"That's amazing," Eleanor said. "But there is no way I could ever have it done. I'm afraid of needles."

"They're so small you can't even feel them," Hamilton insisted.

"I'd like to give it a try," Mr. Wilson said. "It might help that pain in my legs."

"This I have to see," Andrew said.

"Not tonight, though. The Lennon Sisters are performing and

I don't want to miss them," Eleanor said.

"What a great act," Wilson said. "Reminds me of the old days. You know that Lawrence Welk tried to keep those girls looking so innocent and young. I even heard that when they had gotten married and were with child, he had them stand behind a fence to hide their condition."

"Doesn't surprise me. I'm so happy, yet shocked, at how things are these days," I said. "Women sure have more freedom to express themselves. I'm just not sure they need to do it with so few clothes," I said. "No offense, girls, not that I've ever seen you flaunting your bodies like some of the passengers."

"It comes with the territory," Hamilton said.

"It must be hard not to stare," Wilson said. "It's even hard for me and I have no interest in anyone other than my peaches, Eleanor."

"I've just learned not to focus on those thong-wearing beauties. My job depends on it."

"Oh, yes, your policy not to become personally involved with the passengers," I said.

"It's hard, sometimes. I find your daughter positively charming." He laughed. "I don't think I've ever met anyone quite like her before, and she wasn't stalking me like Gloria said, either."

"That's Martha in a nutshell. You should come up to Tawas if you ever get any free time. She wouldn't be a passenger, then."

"Don't tempt me. I just might come up there yet. I have a vacation coming up in a few months."

"That doesn't sound like an appropriate conversation," Gloria said, with drink in hand. "I see you didn't save a seat for me, tonight."

"I didn't know you wanted a seat here. Last night you left when you were invited so I took your name off the list."

Gloria stiffened. Her eyes would have shot sparks from them

if they could have. "I'm sorry about that. I really shouldn't have spoken to you like that. Can I please sit at your table tomorrow night?" She frowned.

"Tomorrow won't work because I am expecting the groom and his groomsmen, who will be boarding in Cozumel for the upcoming wedding, but I'll let you know when I have room. You know you're my favorite guest."

She slightly smiled now. "Thanks, Captain."

"Wow, this certainly is a drama table," I said.

"Don't say I didn't warn you."

Chapter Thirteen

I threw my napkin down on the table after I finished eating. The Maryland chicken was to die for and simply melted in my mouth. I'm not a fan of asparagus, but it tasted great with the lobster sauce. Dessert was strawberry-drizzled cheesecake.

I pushed myself up from the table, wanting to walk off my dinner before the show. Andrew threw an arm around my shoulder and Eleanor made way for the deck with Mr. Wilson, who was in his scooter. There was a nice breeze blowing my hair, ruining the most carefully applied hairspray, but I didn't care. It was just great to be this close to Andrew.

"Oh, no," Mr. Wilson said. "I better roll on down the deck. I feel a huge fart coming."

I snickered as I watched him roll down the deck. I almost felt bad for whoever was near when he let the air go. None of us bothered to stop him, either. We've been in firing range before and didn't care to this time.

The sun had already set, but there were lights on deck, plenty of them about every twenty feet. The pools were also lit up with purple and blue lights. While there might not be that many people in the pool currently, there were certainly passengers in the hot tubs, which is what I'd expect.

Wilson returned and we took a leisurely stroll along the deck. We passed Ricky and Leo, who were chatting it up with a group of young ladies and it was all I could do not to go over them and tell them just what scum I thought they were. I was still shocked about how Ricky was treating Leah and how she allowed it. Even more than that, I wondered why she had ever gone along with it. Why did she have an objection to sleeping with Leo when she obviously didn't care if it was someone else? I mean, she was basically prostituting herself for Ricky, but why? I guess I just would never understand why women would do that, or allow any man to do that to them.

I was about to go over there, too, but Andrew stopped me. "We better get back inside. Eleanor here says if you make her miss the Lennon sisters again, she'll blow a gasket." He paused. "You're not on a case now, are you?"

"Nope. Sure I have questions, but as of now, I guess everything I thought I knew has gone to the birds."

"And what about Ricky and Leo, you're not tailing them?" Andrew asked.

"No, but Ricky has been having Leah, you know—entertaining his clients, and I was told he was trying to recruit some of the staff here for a job. So far it looks like he has been turned down, but it does bother me because I don't think any of the women know what they're getting into until it's too late. Not sure why they just don't leave the first chance they get. Leah promised she'll leave in Florida, but why then and not before? I'm concerned about her. She had a reaction to her medication and the sun. Ricky had to know that she couldn't be in the sun with that medication. I believe he was trying to kill her."

"That hardly sounds like a murder attempt and I highly doubt anyone else would think so, either."

"Fine, I guess you're right, but I'm still worried about Leah."

"Looks like they went inside now, perhaps we should, too."

"Yes, like for the show. You know, the Lennon Sisters," Eleanor said. "You can stalk Ricky inside."

I ignored that barb and followed Eleanor back inside. When we were finally in the atrium, we were waved over by Dorothy and Frank. Him winning money must have agreed with the both of them.

We sat down and the cocktail waitress came over and took our drink order. "You didn't stay long at the captain's table?"

"We decided to have some alone time," Frank said.

"Frank won quite a sum of money today, you know."

"I remember you saying that, but you might want to keep that to yourself," Gloria said, as she was walking past. She stopped and then added, "The last person that told anyone how much he won was robbed."

"Really?" I asked. "Anything else of interest happen on this ship before?"

"Sit, Gloria," Eleanor said. "No reason to be a stranger."

Gloria sat down and said, "Thanks. When it comes to this ship, there have been quite a few crimes, but none as legendary as the Smith robbery. Now that was one for the record books."

"Smith robbery?" I asked.

"They keep it quiet, but Han Smith was a millionaire and was carrying quite the sum of cash. He was one who liked his drinks, though, and while he was watching a show, somebody took it upon themselves to relieve him of his suitcase that was filled with cash."

Eleanor bit her fist. "No!"

"How much did he have?" I asked.

"The rumor circulating didn't establish and amount, but one of the cocktail waitress seemed to know."

"What cocktail waitress was that?" I asked, looking around.

"Jess. She hasn't worked in that position since that incident. The captain wasn't too happy to learn that she had been involved with Han and reassigned her to work the pool area."

"I met Jess and she seems nice."

"Oh, she is, but she was drawn to Han. It might have had something to do with the way he was throwing money around. He was a good tipper and quite the gambler. He always won."

"Did they find out who did it?"

"No, they never did, and it wasn't because they weren't trying. The passengers were all searched, even their bags, when we finally were at the home port, the FBI even took part. The ship was searched, but they came up empty. It was like the money disappeared into thin air."

"That sure is some story to digest," I said.

"Ask Jess if you don't believe me, but don't expect her to talk to you. She signed a confidentially agreement about the incident, like all the staff did. Whatever happened concerning that money was hushed up."

"That makes sense. It's like a black mark against the entire ship and staff."

"I suppose, but I know Captain Hamilton very well and it was really a blow to him, he almost lost his job over the incident."

"What about Han, what happened to him?"

"Went back home from what I know. Sweden, I think."

"I can't believe that money was never found. That explains things."

"Explains what?"

"Just how the lower level is always locked. What do you make of Officer Barber?"

"Irresponsible. He's too swayed by a pretty face and forgets what he's supposed to be doing. I'm just glad that he's not steering the ship."

Me, too, but I wasn't going to tell her that the ship could always be steered from the engine room, if need be.

"Thanks, Gloria. And here I was thinking nothing interesting happens on this ship."

"I know you've been watching that Ricky and Leo, anything you'd care to share?" Gloria asked.

"Nothing to tell, really. I just think that Leah needs to stay away from them. They look like bad news," I said.

"I have to agree with that."

"That's why I've kept an eye on him, but this I will share, he's been trying to hire women so he can prostitute them," I said. "He's over there chatting it up with those women, but I wish I could get the girls away from him."

"Leave it to me," Gloria said. "Watch this."

Gloria moved across the room, starting a conversation with the three women who Ricky and Leo were talking to, and just like magic, they left Ricky and Leo's side, preferring to go wherever Gloria led them. What was her secret? I was finally able to breath again normally. Whatever she said sure worked and for that, I was glad.

Andrew began laughing and I gave him a dead stare. "What is going on with you, Andrew?"

"Just that no matter where we go, intrigue follows you. Why is it that there's always some story about a legendary heist or missing money that you'll no doubt be tearing the ship apart looking for?"

"Just lucky, I guess. It might just lead us to the person responsible for locking up Kacey in that room."

"So, you actually think that a robbery that happened on a completely separate trip is related to a missing girl on this cruise?" Andrew asked.

I shrugged. "I'm not sure just yet, but I'm certainly planning on questioning Jess tomorrow."

Andrew didn't comment on that, instead he focused on the stage where spotlights bounced from floor to ceiling as the Lennon Sisters hit the stage. The entire room was swaying to the singing of the sisters and Andrew moved in closer, throwing an arm around me and drawing me near. This was really what life was about, being in the company of my husband as he held me closer. I smiled at Eleanor, who had her head on Mr. Wilson's shoulder. I guess we both had what we needed with our personal life, and for the moment, I let go of all of my thoughts about how

I'd put all the pieces of the puzzle together in regards to the once-missing Kacey. Tonight was about so much more; it was about love.

Couples made way to the dance floor, including Andrew and me. Even Mr. Wilson and Eleanor were out there. Our waitress had fetched a walker so Wilson could enjoy a dance with this beloved wife. We swayed and sashayed, our dancing feet moving along the floor to the singing of the Lennon Sisters. I could think of no better way to end the night.

I snuggled in closer to Andrew, not wanting to get up when the alarm rang the next morning at seven. Andrew shut it off and asked, "Do you want the shower first, or—"

"It's the perfect day to stay in bed longer." I sighed.

"Really? I'd have thought you'd be raring to go and question that girl about the robbery on that previous cruise."

"Do we have time to do that? Isn't the ship docking in Cozumel today?"

"Yes, but I'm sure you'll want to do the questioning before we go to shore. I'd like to spend a nice day with you without you thinking about this case."

"That's a great idea," I said, as I squirmed away and eased myself on my aching feet. "But I think the shower is roomy enough for two," I hinted.

"Really? Well, I love the sound of that."

I beat Andrew into the bathroom, which gave me time to warm the water before it was ready. I don't know why I was reluctant to share a shower with him. It certainly was nice to have someone scrub my back. It's not like I really can do that all that well myself.

When we were out of the shower, I dressed in yellow Capris and a buttoned-up shirt with yellow flowers that matched the color of my pants. I wore sensible tennis shoes today, too, since we'd be heading to shore later.

Eleanor and Mr. Wilson were waiting for us in the hall and we went down together to have breakfast. The Breakfast Nook was too busy this morning, so we opted to sit at one of the stands with wicker chairs at the counter. A young man was working the grill behind the counter and we were able to watch him cook our food. Oddly enough, he also took the orders with accurate speed. We ordered Arroz Con Huevos since we were near Cozumel now.

I was beginning to get excited when I had spotted the shoreline when we had come off the elevator. I've never been to another country before besides Canada, but that was years ago. In those days you didn't even need a passport like you do now.

Our plates were set down, coffee cups filled, and the cook took another order and was back at the grill with lightning speed.

"I've never seen anyone move that quick before," I said.

"I don't think I've ever had rice and eggs together for breakfast before," Mr. Wilson said. "I won't skimp on the hot sauce, that's for sure," he added, dumping on a healthy portion.

"How on earth do you eat that stuff, Wilson? I'd be suffering all day if I used hot sauce."

"Have you ever tried it?" Wilson asked. "It's not habanera, you know."

"I must admit that I've never used hot sauce before."

"I tried to get her to try it with chicken tenders before, with ranch, of course, but she wouldn't even think about it," Andrew said.

"Fine, I'll add some to my breakfast if it will get you all off my back," I said.

"I never said a word, Agnes," Eleanor insisted. She opened her mouth, but I dumped on the hot sauce before she was able to say anything.

"I was going to say not to use too much, but it looks like it's too late now," she said.

I glanced down at my plate, which had much more hot sauce on it than I had expected to use. I shrugged. There was no way that I'd admit that it was too much. I'd show them that if they could handle hot sauce, I could, too. I picked up my fork and dug in, placing a more-than healthy portion in my mouth. I proceeded to chew, thinking that this wasn't bad at all. It took about a minute before my mouth really began to heat up. Oh, my, this was much worse than I ever could have imagined as the entire roof of my mouth began to burn, my eyes tearing up. Why, this even cleared up my nostrils! I frantically waved a hand before my open mouth now, after I had swallowed my food, of course. I'm not an animal, after all. As luck would have it, I had nothing to drink except for coffee, that surely wouldn't help me out, now.

I finally was able to squeak out, "Water, please."

Eleanor obviously noticed my frantic hand movement as she shouted, "Quick, get my friend some water, she looks about ready to blow."

Blow what I wasn't all the sure, but certainly I'd need a skin replacement in my mouth. That's about when the coughing started. The man left the grill and yanked out a bottle from the refrigerator and handed it to me.

"I wanted water, not milk!"

"It works much better, trust me."

"Does this happen often?" I asked, since he seemed to know what he was talking about, as I proceeded to drink the milk.

"About twenty times a day at least," he said. "Just because this cruise goes to Mexico doesn't mean you have to eat all the spicy things. I had milder sauce in this other bottle, but it looks like you used the one that is much hotter. I don't think that it's all that bad, but if you're not used to it, it can really burn."

"Jose is good like that," a woman said.

When I turned, I was staring into the face of the very woman I wanted to question about the robbery, Jess.

"Gloria told me you'd want to speak with me today, so I thought I'd find you first. She needs more milk, Jose."

I tried not to cough since everyone was now staring at me like I was dying, even though that's exactly how I felt. Instead, in between coughing, I managed to get enough milk in me that my mouth and throat no longer felt quite as bad.

"Looks like I need to put hot sauce on my list of things to never use again."

"I'm sorry I encouraged you to try the hot sauce," Mr. Wilson said.

"Not your fault." I pushed my plate away now. "I don't feel like eating anymore."

"Can't say I blame you there," Jess said. "Look, I need to get to work soon so if you're wanting to ask me any questions, it needs to be now."

"Thanks for finding us, but perhaps we should talk more privately."

"Whatever you'd like, that's probably for the best actually, since the captain doesn't like any of the staff talking about that incident."

I slid out of the chair and Eleanor followed suit. There was a bench not too far away, but it was out of the hearing range of anyone since most everyone on the deck had moved to the back of the ship to watch the coastline get closer and closer.

"What can you tell me about this Han Smith?" I asked.

"He was a great guy, but there were some that said he set the whole thing up ... you know—the robbery?"

"So, how did it all go down?"

"Han was well known on this cruise ship. He routinely takes this cruise."

"I see. I'd like to hear the details of the robbery."

"Fine, but I'm sure that Gloria might have hinted that I spent some time with Han. I broke a few of the ships rules there, but honestly, I fell for the guy. I didn't expect to be in the middle of an investigation when it happened. The FBI even thought that I was in cahoots with Han, but nothing could be further from the truth."

"What kind of business was this Han in?"

"He's a millionaire and carries cash from the states to Mexico for his father. He's made this trip many times."

"Bringing cash from the United States seems suspect to me. There has to be some illegal activity going on there."

"I really couldn't say, since Han never told me that it was."

"Men are good at concealing things sometimes," I said.

"Well, I spent most of that day with Han since I had the day off and the captain was tied up with an inspection and many passengers weren't even on the ship, they were in Cozumel."

"I see. So when did Han realize the money was gone?"

"The next morning. We were together that whole night and Han couldn't have been involved."

"What if the money was gone longer? He might have been using you for an alibi," I suggested.

"I just can't believe it happened. Captain Hamilton had this ship torn apart looking for that money, but it wasn't located and searches were conducted."

"Did anyone ever think that it might have been hidden on the ship somewhere?"

"I can't say, but all I know is that the FBI searched all of the passengers, even the ones who were at shore. I can't imagine where that money had gone."

"So, that money was never located. What happened to you for your involvement with a passenger?"

"I was on suspension, but Captain Hamilton went to bat for me. I had to give up my job as cocktail waitress and work on deck activities, though, but I'm just happy to be working on the ship. I plan on going to college next fall and need all the money I can get."

"Have you seen Han since the robbery?"

"Not a chance. There's no way that I'm ruining my life by seeing Han after I promised the captain that I'd stay away. I also knew the FBI was watching me after the robbery and that did bother me, even though I know I kind of did that to myself by seeing Han."

"Weren't you discrete?" Eleanor wanted to know.

"We tried to be, but I was stupid in love, I guess. What really bothered me was how so many people were so ready to throw me under the bus. I'm not sure if whoever did this works closely with Han, since the FBI interviewed them all. I just assumed that somehow that money did get off this ship. I'm just at a loss as to how that would happen."

"That sure is some story," I said. "I can't imagine that the money is still here. There might have been some accomplices that helped that money to disappear. It wouldn't surprise me if it was someone employed on this ship."

"That's been the ongoing theme, but the FBI checked everyone out. I'm sure if they had anything on anyone, they'd have moved in for an arrest."

"Thanks, Jess. If you can think of anything else, let us know."

Jess gave me a strange look. "Sure, but I'm not sure why you'd be concerned about that since it happened last year."

"Last year?" I asked. "From the way Gloria sounded, I thought it wasn't all that long ago."

"Gloria is a sweet old lady, but sometimes she gets a little mixed up with the details. She's also a notorious gossip." Jess winked.

"The captain said as much."

"She acts like she's his mother sometimes, with the way she tries to keep women away from him. I almost think she might have a crush on him."

"That explains a lot," Eleanor said. "I think Gloria is very insightful, which is never a bad thing. Us older folks are like that.

I'm sure plenty of people back home appreciate an alert neighbor. They're the first ones who will check up on a neighbor if they leave their garage door open when they don't ordinarily do that, or if a toddler wanders outside without their parents realizing it."

Jess laughed. "All of those things would be good. I wasn't used to people watching me the way they do here, but the staff here looks after each other. We're a family in many ways," Jess said. "But honestly, I'm originally from New York and we don't get all that involved with our neighbors there."

I nodded. "Being from Michigan is a little different than that for sure. We can and will talk to anyone and we don't see anything wrong with that. Nobody ever looks at me like I'm crazy when I talk to myself, either."

"She means talking out loud. Agnes thinks better that way. She sometimes likes to spout off her irritation at people, under her breath most times, like when she deals with our Sheriff Peterson."

"Oh, you don't get along with the local sheriff?"

"I get along with him much better than I once did. I think we just like to get under each other's skin. To be expected when you investigate crimes. The law likes to do their own investigations and don't much appreciate our interference at times."

"I bet you two are a ton of fun back home," Jess said. "I've enjoyed our talk, but I really need to get back to work now. You know my grandmother isn't all that much different than you. She's not the type to keep the bad words in, if you know what I mean."

"I bet we'd love her," Eleanor said. "Thanks again, dear, for answering our questions."

I gave Eleanor one of my looks. "Yes, we just love a good story, especially when it's a true-crime one."

I watched as Jess left and sighed. "Well, I guess that story certainly doesn't apply all that much to our investigation, but it sure was interesting."

Andrew locked eyes with me as he drowned the last of his coffee. "Good, so that means we can enjoy ourselves in Cozumel today."

Chapter Fourteen

After breakfast, we went to where you had to wait for your turn to go ashore in Cozumel. We were each handed a card with a number for the tour we selected.

"I wished we had picked the Mayan ruins," Eleanor said.

"Me, too, but that's a two-hour bus trip and I don't think it would accommodate Mr. Wilson that well."

Leotyne waved from the shadows of an awning.

Martha waltzed over. "What tour are you on?"

"We're doing shopping and lunch."

"That sounds boring," Martha said. "Denise set us up to go scuba diving. Luckily, I took a scuba class last summer, but you can't see all that much in Lake Huron. I'm looking forward to taking some underwater photographs, too."

"You have an underwater camera?" I asked, surprised.

"Well, no, but Captain Hamilton was kind enough to loan me one. He's really a nice man when you get to know him," Martha said.

"I never thought he wasn't," I said. "I like Captain Hamilton."

Denise Munson waved. She was a real genuine person. It was just too bad that she had to deal with that bad apple Ruby as the leader of the group. Neither Ruby nor Pearl were with Denise today, so I figured they really had been staying in the cabin after Denise became angry the other night. Violet and Lenore were here, though, making it four of them going ashore, since Leotyne clearly wasn't accompanying them.

I looked around now. Dorothy and Frank Alton weren't here

and must not be going ashore either, but the way they acted last night after the Lennon Sisters set had ended made me think that they might just stay in their cabin, acting like the honeymooners we were supposed to be. I did feel a little badly that I hadn't spent all that much time with Andrew, but he didn't seem to mind all that much. I loved the way that man rolled with the twists and turns of my investigative activities.

Kacey nodded her head at me when I spotted her with the rest of the wedding party, including the parents of the bride and groom. I honestly couldn't wait until I met the groom. It's always strange when you know someone who's getting married and you haven't met the other party. I put a mental image in my mind of a tall man with dark hair who would compliment Liz well since she was such a cute girl. I could only imagine it would make any new bride a little nervous if she were separated from her future husband, especially one who was partying with his friends in Mexico before the wedding. I guess I've watched too many Hangover movies to see that as a good thing.

Our numbers weren't called first, or even second, although Martha and the Sunrise Side Lifelong Learning gang were one of the first ones who piled into the small ferryboat.

While we waited for our turn, Lemonade was passed around and we enjoyed it. Mr. Wilson was sitting on a bench since he'd be using a walker for this excursion today.

Kacey came over and said hello in person, now. "How are things going, Agnes and Eleanor?"

"Fine, and how about you? I hope you haven't had any problems since you returned to your friends."

"Not at all, except for that creepy man who keeps following us."

"Oh, and which one is that?"

"The same one that you keep following."

"The one with Leah, or—"

"His friend, but that one I don't care for that much, either. I think it's horrible the way Leah has been treated by that boyfriend of hers."

"Ricky isn't my favorite, either, and his friend Leo is even farther up the creep scale, if you ask me."

Kacey glanced around. "At least they're not waiting to go to shore."

"Don't jinx it," Eleanor said. "It would be just like them to show up. Stay with your friends today. I'd hate to see anything happen to you."

"What my faithful friend means is that we wouldn't want to see anything *else* happen to you. You've been through enough already."

"I second that."

"Come along, dear," Pat Busch said to Kacey. "Our number is up next."

Pat put a hand on Kacey's back and led her back to the wedding party and I didn't like the way that woman interrupted us when we were speaking. Truth was that I was worried about Kacey and couldn't quit thinking that something might befall the girl.

After ten minutes, our numbers were called and we filed in behind the wedding party members, who were obviously going the same place as us, or at least ashore at the same time.

Mr. Wilson was helped aboard first, since he was the only one who really needed the extra help. I almost felt that some of the wedding party minded that we went aboard the ferry first. It wasn't like they said anything. It was more of a feeling I had. I'm sure Liz wanted to be considered the most important person here, since she would be getting married tomorrow, but she was on a cruise, after all, and things just couldn't revolve only around her.

Kacey walked by us and leaned down slightly and said, "Don't be offended. Pat is a little pushy. She just wants her daughter to have the perfect wedding."

I nodded and Kacey went back to her friends.

"She's such a nice girl," Mr. Wilson said. "Reminds me a little of my granddaughter Millicent. I sure wish Millicent would meet a man. I worry about that girl."

"We've been talking about that for a long time," I said. "But I'd hate to introduce her to anybody. If he broke her heart, I don't think I'd ever forgive myself."

"It's none of our business and we need to stay out of her life," Eleanor insisted.

"Probably right," Wilson said. "She does work too much and I'm going to insist she take a vacation when I get back."

When the ferry took off, it was all I could do not to upchuck on the spot. The water was rather rough today and I squeezed Andrew's hand tightly.

"If I had known this ride would be so rocky, I wouldn't have decided to go ashore."

Andrew handed me a pill and I promptly tossed it back with a hard swallow, declining Eleanor's offer to fetch a bottle of water. The truth was that I'd much rather not ingest anything else right now for fear of losing it completely.

When the ferry finally docked, I was the first to disembark, even before Mr. Wilson. I about dropped and kissed the ground as my legs were quite shaky now. Andrew wouldn't allow me to sit down just yet, as he led me away from the dock and we sat in a bench over-looking the shops.

"Don't even look at the ocean right now. Give yourself some time to get your bearings before we go shopping."

"I'm so sorry, Andrew. I had no idea that I'd feel so bad."

He squeezed my hand. "Don't worry. I'm sure that pill will kick in and you'll be just fine."

Eleanor and Mr. Wilson walked up the street and once I felt better, I allowed Andrew to lead me up after them. I didn't see the wedding party and figured that they were searching for the groom about now. I was just dying to see him myself, along with the merry band of groomsmen.

We took our time wandering in and out of shops, many of which had skull-looking things. The shop girl must have seen my expression and explained, "They represent the Day of the Dead."

"Day of the what?" Eleanor asked.

"It's a holiday where we gather with our families. We pray and remember loved ones who have died. We celebrate it in the fall."

I had to remember that this was indeed a different culture and that most people in Mexico were Catholics. Even in the United States, people of Mexican descent honored family members who had passed away. You had to admire that.

"That's very interesting," I said. "These skulls look so scary to me, is all I meant. I meant no disrespect."

"I know you didn't, not to worry."

"You speak good English," Eleanor said.

"Yes, I was raised by my grandparents and they traveled to the states often. They wanted me to learn and speak English well. I know it's not like most of the people I know, but my grandparents are a little unconventional."

"By that, she means that we enjoy traveling and having fun," said an older man, as he walked forward. "We made sure our granddaughter got a proper education. She's going to medical school in California in the fall."

"Wow, great news."

The girl shook her head. "But Papa, I need to stay here and help you run this store."

"Nonsense," said an older woman, who was on a ladder dusting. "You'll do us proud. We could use more doctors in Cozumel, if you decide to come back after you're a doctor."

"Why wouldn't I?"

"Because you might meet a nice young man and get married is why."

The young lady gave me a strange look and I knew this must have been an ongoing argument, so I agreed with the grandmother. "She's right, love finds you when you least expect it. We just were married back home," I said.

The woman came down the ladder and gave me a hug. "How nice to see someone my age get married."

"What? We've been married since we were sixteen," her husband said.

"I meant that not too many people our age get married. Most of my widow friends have given up on men and love. You should never give up on love. There's no greater thing in the world."

We wandered around the shop as the granddaughter and grandparents continued to discuss the topic of love, but also the importance of waiting until she had a proper education, first.

Before we left the shop, I bought a pink sundress that was plentiful in the material department, which I loved. It would be the perfect thing to wear when I wanted to be comfortable at home.

When we finally left the shop, Eleanor said, "I loved the store owners. They sounded like a real hoot. You don't see many people speaking English in Mexico as well as they do."

"Well, they are store owners who get plenty of American visitors. I think that's more than a good reason to speak better English."

We hit just about every shop on the strip, then finally found a restaurant to eat. We sat inside and it was quite hot, but there were several ceiling fans overhead.

The waitress came over, wearing a multi-colored skirt and peasant-type blouse, and took our order, bringing us back bottled water. I breathed in deeply of the spices that were being sprinkled on the food that was cooking. It didn't take long before plates of grilled steak and chicken, with rice and hand-made tortillas, were brought to our table. The food was very spicy, but tasted wonderful.

I heard giggling and when I turned, the wedding party was entering the restaurant, with four young men, a few of them with beer bellies. That brought a smile to my face for a moment, as I said, "I wonder which one is the groom."

"It would be funny if it was the one with the beer gut," Eleanor said.

When one of them threw an arm around Liz, I took him as the groom. While he was quite slim, he also wore glasses and looked to be more of the nerd type. Honestly, I couldn't imagine him and Liz together. While she did allow the affection he was showing her, I almost wondered if she was marrying him because she really loved him, or if she just loved what he'd become one day. Ever since the way Liz and her mother had spoken at the captain's table, I just couldn't like either of them. There was more to life than money, in my opinion.

Kacey smiled and walked over. "Hello again." She eyed up our bags and said, "Looks like you've been shopping. I hope you have at least one of those skulls in your bags. You can't get them like that back in the states."

"So, the groom did show up?"

"Yes, I don't understand why he showed up, actually. I love Liz, but I doubt her commitment to Brady."

"I'm shocked to hear you say that."

"I am, too, but ever since my little excursion, I think of life in a whole new way. I went to high school with Liz, but I never realized how superficial she really is until this trip. Her family paid for my trip, but honestly, I was shocked she asked me to be her matron of honor, since she has so many more friends to choose from."

I didn't know what to say. "She obviously made the right choice. Why did you agree to be the matron of honor in the first place?"

"I'm ashamed to admit that the free cruise lured me in, but I was a little surprised that her parents were so willing to pay my way."

"Kacey," Pat Busch said. "Come on back to our group, now. I'm sure the old folks would rather be left alone."

"What old folks are you talking about?" Eleanor said.

"Take care, those are fighting words with Eleanor," I explained.

Pat backed away now, with her arm interlaced with Kacey's.

"What is going on there, I wonder?" Eleanor said. "Why is she constantly pulling Kacey away from us?"

"She sure is pushy is all I can say, and possibly a little controlling."

"You think?"

"She might just be worried about Kacey straying too far from the wedding party," Andrew said. "It's easy to get lost in Cozumel."

I wish I could agree with Andrew here, but I couldn't stop myself from thinking about how Pat looked at Kacey. "Or, they don't want her to go missing again."

"She should be fine, since it looks like Ricky and Leo stayed on the ship," Eleanor said.

"Yes, right." Until Eleanor mentioned it, I had all but forgotten about Ricky and Leo, my prime suspects in Kacey's disappearance. I'd just be happy when we were back on board safely. I tried not to think what it would be like to be back on the ferry. I just hoped it wouldn't be quite as bad as the way here.

We finished our meal and I was almost disappointed that I wasn't sitting closer to the wedding party so I could eavesdrop, but alas, it was not meant to be. I was very curious about the groom, Brady. I don't know why I was so focused on the wedding party. It must be because of Kacey's disappearance, I rationalized. Why did I have the impression that she still might be in danger?

Chapter Fifteen

I was helped back onto the deck of the cruise ship by Andrew and I promptly sat on the nearby bench, trying to steady the rolling of my stomach. The way back from Cozumel wasn't any better on the ferry than the way there, thanks to the choppy waves. That's something I'm not all that used to since back home, Lake Huron doesn't nearly have the waves that the ocean can muster up. Sure, we have our storms and at the point where the lighthouse is located, it's very windy and the water can get very rough. I guess I never paid all that much attention to it, though, since I've never been in a boat when the weather was like that. We paid attention to gale warnings and such back home.

Dr. Gordon strode over to me, putting a cool cloth on the back of my neck.

"What's that going to do?"

"It will help you feel better, I hope." He winked.

"How did you know I was sick?"

"The captain of the ferry called and told me. Somebody should have warned you about how it would go on the ferry with these rough seas today."

"I wish they had, so at least I would have known what to expect, but I probably would have gone anyway. This is my honeymoon and I don't want to ruin it for everyone."

My stomach quit rolling for the moment and I had to admit that the cool cloth did help out somewhat.

"Don't be silly, Agnes," Andrew said. "We won't be going ashore at any of the other stops. I don't want you to be miserable on this trip."

I smiled up at Andrew. "Thanks, I think I'm feeling a little better now. I'm ready to go to our room."

"Don't be silly, give it more time before you attempt that," the doctor said.

"Fetch my scooter, would you man? Agnes can use it to get to her room. I can use the walker," Mr. Wilson said.

Before I had a chance to say anything, Eleanor went to fetch the scooter and drove it back, helping me aboard. I felt like a cripple using this. It's not that people my age didn't need to use apparatuses like this; I just didn't want to be one of them. I was fighting old age with all that was in me. Sure, if I had to, I would, but I really didn't have more than an aching hip or knee on occasion.

I zoomed toward the elevator and I could see why Wilson did that. It was fun with the wind blowing my hair about. Once I was back at our room, I climbed off without any assistance and entered my room. Andrew followed me in, but Eleanor and Mr. Wilson headed over to their room for some relaxation, no doubt. That's all I ever wanted to know about the goings on over there.

I took a quick shower, which helped me feel even better. When I looked in the mirror afterward, I was shocked at how red my face, and especially my nose, looked. I had gotten quite the sunburn and I guess I had forgotten all about the sunscreen. I had my mind on other things like shopping. It's so strange how you don't even know you have a sunburn until later. I worried about how badly Eleanor might have burned, since she had much fairer skin than me.

I changed clothing and I noticed Andrew's nose was slightly red from the sun. He had a button-up shirt on that revealed his tanned skin beneath, since he rarely burned. I had to look away or we'd never make it anywhere else today.

I was startled out of my thoughts by the sound of a knock at the door. Andrew answered it and Captain Hamilton walked in with a man I hadn't yet met. Was he the engineer who Hamilton had told me was coming aboard in Cozumel?

"What can I help you with, Captain? Was there another crime committed?"

"I certainly hope not. This is Darnell Dobson, the engineer I told you about."

"Oh, of course, but you could have introduced him to me later."

Darnell's face was quite pale. "Did you happen to take anything out of the suitcase and forget to put it back?"

"No, I don't think so, why?"

"It's just that there was a very special key inside, too. It was a golden key."

"Golden key?" Andrew raised a brow. "Do you know anything about this, Agnes?"

"No, but that bag wasn't exactly secured when I found it at the airport. It might have dropped out there."

Darnell leaned against the captain, who eased him into a chair. "Are you okay, Darnell?" Hamilton asked.

"I-I don't think so. My goose is cooked for sure, now. That's a very special key."

I knew this was the time to hand it over, but not until I knew exactly what that key was for. "It's strange having a blueprint of the ship in your suitcase and I don't know many men who have a floral suitcase," I began. "I really should call my son Stuart, he works for the FBI, you know. This sounds like something Homeland Security would love to know about. I hope you're not planning to hijack the ship."

"He's the engineer of this ship," Hamilton said. "He designed the ship!"

"Then why the floral suitcase?"

"Because people know who I am and my blueprints have been stolen before. I use the floral suitcase to throw them off, I even have my secretary check it in for me."

My shoulders dropped now. "Oh, but what about the golden key, what is that for?"

"It unlocks the floor panel in the bridge. There is an electrical unit that needs to be replaced," Darnell said.

"Why wasn't that fixed before the ship went out to sea?"

"Because I missed my flight. If that electrical unit isn't replaced and soon, there's no telling what might happen."

"But the ship can be run from the engine room," I said.

"Not if that circuit blows," Hamilton said. "We've already lost partial communications."

"Then why did you allow anyone to go ashore?"

"I'm not about to ruin the cruise for everyone. Besides, Darnell needed to get aboard somehow."

"Prove it to me, then," I said.

Captain Hamilton's face turned red. "Prove *what* to you?"

"That the key opens a panel on the bridge and not something else."

"Agnes, if you have the key, you need to hand it over," Andrew said. "This is serious."

"What do you think the key opens?" Hamilton asked.

"Well, I heard the story about Han Smith and how he had a large amount of money stolen while on one of the cruises. I figured that the key opens a secret compartment where the money was hidden by whoever took it. I'm sure the FBI searching the ship made it impossible for anyone to retrieve the money until a later date."

Captain Hamilton and Darnell stared at each other for a moment, then Hamilton said, "So, you think someone hid that money on the ship a year ago and they weren't planning to retrieve the money until now?" He laughed.

"Don't laugh, she's deadly serious about this," Andrew said. "She an investigator back home and if she thinks that's what happened, she's probably right."

"Come along to the bridge, then," Hamilton said. "We can prove where the key goes."

I waited until the captain and the engineer left before I retrieved the key from where I had hidden it, keeping it safely in my pocket for the moment. Only then did I join Darnell and Captain Hamilton outside where Eleanor and Wilson were looking on, puzzled.

"What's going on here, Agnes?" Eleanor asked.

"The captain says he can prove the golden key opens a floor panel. He claims an electrical unit needs to be replaced. We're going to check it out, now."

"I'm so coming," Eleanor said, moving toward the elevator, with Wilson and Andrew following closely.

Eleanor smiled widely at Ruby and Pearl as we passed by them on the main deck, she even fingered Mr. Wilson's sleeve to let Ruby know that she wasn't about to give up Wilson to anyone.

"Do you think it's wise to rile that woman?" I asked Eleanor.

"Sorry, I guess I couldn't help myself."

Once we were all in the bridge, Theo and Gunner were trying to move a panel on the floor with a screwdriver.

"What do you think you're doing?" Darnell shouted. "You're going to get electrocuted doing that, even with that electrical unit on the fritz, there is plenty of raw power down there. Who knows what sort of catastrophe might happen."

I stared at the keyhole and produced the golden key, handing it to Darnell, who inserted it, carefully turning the key in the lock until a click was heard, then lifting the panel. "See, just like I told you."

Captain Hamilton called down to the engine room, asking for the repair technicians to report to the bridge to replace the electrical panel.

When Hamilton hung up, I sighed. "I just don't understand why that key wouldn't be on the ship the entire time if that's what it's for."

"It was, but somehow it became lost and I had to fly all the way to New York to retrieve the blueprint and key so that we could replace that unit," Darnell said. "The owner is a little eccentric and wouldn't email a copy of the blueprint to the captain. He has all the spare keys at his home and refuses to allow the captain to have the spare key here."

"That seems dumb, but if the electric panel was that bad, it should have been replaced sooner. Why, anything could have happened that might have endangered the passengers."

"I tried to tell the owner that, but Gerald doesn't like his captains telling him anything. He thinks he knows what's best," Hamilton explained.

"Well, he was wrong this time around. Please speak to him about the matter or I'll show up at the owner's house myself and tell him exactly what I think about his policies. He should trust the captains who run the ships and if he doesn't, he needs to park his behind on all the cruises to oversee things," Eleanor said in a huff.

Leave it to Eleanor to tell it like it is.

"I'm sorry, Captain Hamilton, for thinking you're hiding details about where that money might be and what the golden key was for."

"Don't look at me, Captain," Andrew said. "This is the first I've even heard about blueprints or the golden key."

"I meant to tell you, but I knew you wouldn't have approved of me keeping the blueprints and key from the captain."

"I told you to hand over that suitcase to begin with, but I guess it's all worked out."

"And you really don't know where that stolen money is?" I asked the captain.

"No, and it wasn't from a lack of trying. The FBI even swept the ship."

"Does your son really work for the FBI, or is that a story you made up?" Darnell asked.

"No, it's true. I've only recently reconnected with my son and him being part of the FBI was a complete shock to me. I'd sure love to give him a call and find out the details of the search of this ship. I can't help but wonder if the money is still here."

"Keep your thoughts to yourself. I don't have to guess where you heard about that robbery to begin with. Sometimes I'd like to put Gloria off this ship permanently."

"Don't blame her. She's a senior citizen and gossiping is what we do. It's not like we can do much of anything else."

"Not according to the way Gloria moves on the dance floor, but you're right, I shouldn't blame Gloria for spreading the rumor. I just would hate to have all the passengers find out and tear the ship apart, looking for it."

"What about us?" I asked. "If we could get a master key, I'd be satisfied to look below decks. I promise that we won't tear the ship apart."

"That would be against policy, but since it seems we already have a missing master key, I'm sure it would be all right if you have one. I trust that you won't tear up the ship looking for the money. I'm quite sure it's long gone."

Captain Hamilton removed a master key from the cabinet and pressed it into my hand. "Good luck."

"Hey, what about my suitcase?" I asked.

"I'll send it to your room later," Darnell said. "I was so worried about finding this key that I had forgotten all about bringing your suitcase to your room."

"That's fine. I can wait until tomorrow, I suppose."

We left the bridge, but we hadn't gotten very far when Andrew said, "Don't think that I have forgotten about how you lied to me about the contents of that suitcase."

"I didn't lie exactly, I just didn't tell you."

"That's the same as lying, Agnes," Eleanor said. "She didn't even tell me right away, but I'm sure she was just trying to sort things out. I'm sure she'd have told you eventually."

"Like when the ship blew up?"

"Nothing quite as dramatic as that."

"And I suppose you'll be leaving now to check out below decks for treasure."

"Stolen money," I said. "And that's not in my plans right now. So far on this cruise, everything I thought I knew turned out to be easily explained."

"Perhaps that's an omen that you shouldn't try and find a case that needs solving."

"Well, I still don't know how Kacey happened to get locked in a room below decks when you'd need a master key, or who might have done such a thing or why."

"She's back with her friends, safe and sound, so that's hardly something to be worried about," Andrew said.

"And Kacey will be busy with Liz and Brady's wedding tomorrow. I hope we'll be able to attend — unless we can't. I wonder if we need an invitation," Eleanor said.

I heard a throat being cleared and Brady stood there with an invitation. "Liz wants you to attend our wedding. I heard about how you helped find Kacey when she disappeared that day."

"Not sure what happened with that, but we just tried to help."

"We weren't that much help, though, since Kacey turned up unharmed," Eleanor added. "Thanks for the invitation. I'm sure you and Liz will be a very happy couple."

"How did you meet?" I asked.

"Why don't you come into the dining room so we can sit down and have a little chat. From the looks of it, you both are quite red already."

"Go on ahead," Andrew said. "Mr. Wilson and I are moseying to the casino for a few hours. Meet us there after you talk to the groom."

I gave Andrew a kiss and Eleanor and I followed Brady into one of the smaller dining rooms, where only the groomsmen were. Brady motioned to us to sit and he introduced us to his part of the wedding party. Richard and Philip were the trimmer ones of the group, and Buzz was the best man and Gus was the last groomsmen, both of them sporting beer bellies.

"Wow, what colorful names you all have, but I'd love to hear how Brady and Liz met."

"We met at one of her father's hardware stores. I worked there after school every day and she never told her dad that I spent most of my time studying. Liz is good at getting her way and had no qualms about asking me out."

Eleanor laughed. "I just love a woman who knows what she wants and goes after it."

"Things moved along pretty quickly and soon we were inseparable, when I wasn't studying, that is. It was much harder to win over her dad."

"It would seem he'd be thrilled that his daughter was dating a man who was interested in becoming a doctor."

"I'm not sure that's what I knew back then, but I did plan to go to college. Liz was the one who suggested that I take up medicine."

"So, you don't want to be a doctor?" I asked.

"I do, but my father is a lawyer and I had wanted to follow in his footsteps, but once I began doing my pre-med, I was hooked. Of course it's quite expensive and I'm trying to find a way to pay for school without asking my father. I want to prove it to him that I can do it without his help. I also want to let Liz's father know I'll be a good provider."

"Medical school is quite lengthy," I said. "I wish you good luck in the future and I'm sure you'll be a good doctor one day." Buzz busted out laughing and I asked, "Did I say something wrong?"

"Not at all," Brady said. "Buzz thinks all this medical school stuff is a waste of time."

"That's why we took him to Cozumel," Buzz said. "Brady

needs to have some fun before he says his, 'I do's.' We used to have so much fun."

"You can still have fun after you're married," I insisted. "But some things do change."

"Or they should," Eleanor said. "Brady will be plenty busy with school to have room left for much more. Why didn't you wait until later to get married? Certainly there wasn't a rush?"

"Liz insisted and her mother was all gung ho about it, too."

"No surprise there," slipped out of my lips.

"Agnes means that mothers feel much better when their children leave the nest and get married."

"She won't exactly be leaving the nest too soon, not with me in college. We agreed that she wouldn't come along until later. I really need to focus on my studies."

"Sounds like you have put everything into perspective," I said.

"Trying to. So what's your story, ladies?"

"We're just your run of the mill retires, other than the fact that we just married our men, and we're on our honeymoon now," Eleanor said, as she stood and stretched. "We should go now and leave you to spend your last night as a single man. Don't get yourself into any trouble."

I followed Eleanor out into the sunlight, now. "Brady seems like a nice man, but I'm not sure why he's so hard pressed to get married so soon."

"Liz's father owns a chain of hardware stores. Perhaps Brady thinks if he marries Liz, then he'll get some help for college."

"Not the way he sounded, but since it was Liz's idea for him to go into medical school, it's the least her father could do." I laughed.

CHAPTER SIXTEEN

Eleanor and I were enjoying a quiet dinner in one of the smaller dining rooms with our husbands. Martha had popped in to say she'd be turning in early. Apparently, she was exhausted from her scuba diving. Leotyne had been pretty quiet on this trip, but she did warn us, "Be careful, girls, your instincts may have led you astray, but your hearts are true."

Like always when it came to Leotyne, it was yet another riddle that didn't make any sense. Not sure how she knew we were wrong about anything on this cruise since we have barely spoken to her. I'm not even sure why she came; she hasn't been in the sun once that I know of. It's not like she's a vampire or anything, just a Romanian fortune teller who rolled into the Tawas city campground in a big black camper one day and hasn't left since. I used to be frightened of her, but on occasion, I did seek out her help. But it was everything but help. Eleanor and I don't really need any help; we figure out things for ourselves, eventually.

Andrew stared at me over the glow of the candlelight. "It's nice to have a private dinner, for a change."

"I agree."

"He means the four of us, I think," Eleanor said to Wilson.

"I think he's pretending that we're alone," I said.

"I don't mind Eleanor and Wilson. I rather enjoy their company. Mr. Wilson cleaned up at craps today. Who knew you could throw a dice like that."

"It's good to know I haven't lost it. I haven't played that in years. Eleanor doesn't care for the casino."

"That's not true," Eleanor said. "I've always wanted to go to Vegas, but it's never been in the cards."

"We could always take a side trip on our way home," Andrew suggested.

"That's nowhere on the way home, but I wouldn't mind stopping there, either," I said.

Our food was brought and we dug in, leaving all the talk of Vegas for another day. I thought about Leah and vowed that I'd check to see if she was still in the infirmary. I was so absorbed with going into Cozumel that I had almost forgotten about Ricky and Leo being our number one suspects in Kacey's disappearance. If anyone would kidnap a woman, it had to be them. It still bothered me that Leah had been abused at the hands of those men. If only I could have been more help to her. Sure, I had tried to convince Leah to leave Ricky before we got back to Florida, but she seemed to be resistant to the idea.

After our candlelight dinner, Andrew and Mr. Wilson told us they'd meet us in the atrium for dancing, which sounded just fine to me. I did want to stroll along the deck and see if I could spot Ricky or Leo, and Leah, of course. We hadn't walked very far before Leah raced toward us, tears streaming down her face.

"Oh, Agnes," she wailed. "I-I was looking for Ricky and h-he's in the hot tub, and he's not moving!"

We rushed to the other side of the deck. It was dark outside now, but once we reached the hot tub, Ricky and Leo were in there, both of them face down in the water. "Get help!" I shouted. I was about to dive into the water and move Ricky and Leo out of the hot tub, but Leah shouted for me to stop.

"When I found them here, I heard an electrical currant crackling. It smells like burnt electrical cords."

I nodded. "You're right. Get the captain and we'll wait right here."

Leah left and I stared at the bodies of Ricky and Leo, all the color leaving my face. "Here were go again," I said. "Our main suspects in Kacey's disappearance appear to be dead, but this time, we're so going to stay put. I don't want these bodies to disappear, too."

Eleanor wrinkled her nose and led me toward the rail. "Are you thinking what I am, that Leah might just be responsible, here?"

"I thought that, but if it's electrical, she might not be involved at all. It's not like she could set that up. I wonder if when the engineer replaced the electrical unit, it caused this to happen?"

"I guess we'll find out, there's the captain."

Captain Hamilton and several members of security rushed forward. "I smell burnt wires," I said. "Can you cut off the power to that hot tub? What if they died because of the wiring?"

"I hope you're not suggesting that us replacing the electrical unit in the bridge is responsible for electrocuting them?"

"You said it, not me, Captain Hamilton, but I highly doubt what you were doing in the bridge has anything to do with these men."

Captain Hamilton called on his two-way radio, asking for the power to be cut for hot tub number ten. Not only was the hot tub cut off, but all the lights within twenty feet in either direction. Ricky and Leo were pulled from the hot tub and we stood back, turning Leah away from the bodies.

"You don't need to see this," I said.

"Who found them?" Hamilton asked.

"I did," Leah cried. "I was looking for Ricky and Leo everywhere when they never showed up for dinner."

"Did you see what happened, Agnes and Eleanor?"

"No, Leah showed us where Ricky and Leo were. If she hadn't stopped me, I might have been electrocuted myself."

"What makes you think they've been electrocuted?"

"It's obvious — burnt wires and you can smell them, as well. I had thought they were responsible for Kacey's disappearance, but now it couldn't be them, after all."

"So, you're batting negative three?" Hamilton asked. "And Liz has been searching for Kacey all night, since she never showed up for dinner."

"She's missing, again? I should have known it. If Ricky and Leo weren't responsible, then who is?"

"You should leave now and take Leah with you. We'll be investigating the malfunction of this hot tub."

I didn't have a problem leaving now. I had to question the wedding party about Kacey. That feeling I was having about Kacey being in danger wasn't wrong at all. With Liz and Brady's wedding tomorrow, it couldn't have happened at a worse time.

It took quite a few trips in and out of dining rooms to locate the wedding party that had split up, searching for Kacey. When I finally found Pat Busch with her daughter Liz, we made our way over there.

"What happened?" I asked.

"I got into an argument with Kacey," Liz said. "She called me superficial and I'm not. I'll admit that I'm far from perfect, but I'm not marrying Brady for the money, because he doesn't have any."

"Were you the one who suggested he go to medical school to begin with?" I asked.

"Yes, but it's much more lucrative than being a lawyer. It certainly never helped his father out that much. He was disbarred for fraud and if it wasn't for my father, he wouldn't even be able to afford his pre-med."

"And did it ever occur to you that you're being singled out because of your family's business? Brady might be using you to pay for medical school and could drop you later. It happens."

Liz frowned now, like she was absorbing what I was trying to tell her. "I guess I never thought about that. Brady even suggested that I stay with my parents, that I'd be too much of a distraction if I lived with him while he was in med school."

"So, why are you getting married?"

"I-I don't know, but I have to find Kacey. I'm lost without her."

"She told me she was surprised that you even picked her to be your matron of honor."

"That's true, but there's nobody I'd rather have serve in the role. All of my other friends aren't like Kacey. She's honest and genuine. I guess that's why she told me off like she did today, but I'm really not like that. I mean, I have said things or acted like all that matters to me is being a doctor's wife, but I have had my doubts about his true intentions. He's asked me about Kacey's family, too. I wish I had just kept my mouth shut, but her family, or her father, is legendary. He was one of the men who people say might have been involved in the theft of Han Smith's money that was stolen from this very ship a year ago."

"I really don't see how that makes him legendary."

"He's a thief and pulled off a few heists, even went to prison for ten years, but he was released and was on this cruise when Han Smith was robbed."

"Where is Kacey's father now?"

"I'm not sure. Kacey told me she hasn't spoken to him in years. Her father's past has been an embarrassment to her and a black mark against the entire family. Back in high school, she was shunned, but her family wasn't a concern for me. Kacey is a great person … and she's the sweetest person I've ever known. Since high school, she hasn't told anyone about her father's past."

"So, Brady was interested in Kacey's father, but why is that a concern for you?"

"Because she thinks Kacey might be used to get her father to come clean about where the money is," Eleanor said.

"I wanted to hear Liz say that," I said. "I've put that part together already. Kacey lied about going off with a man that first day when she disappeared," I informed her.

Liz's eye widened. "I know. She told me that she didn't want to worry me. I'm just not sure why she kept it from me."

"I suppose you'll have to ask her that yourself if we find her," Eleanor said.

"Right now I'm worried that someone is holding her somewhere to get at her father, using her to force him to reveal where the money is. Threatening to kill her, even," I said.

Liz bit down on her fist. "We have to find her and quick."

"When was the last time you spoke with Brady?"

"Before dinner, but he never showed up to eat with me. That seemed strange, since we're getting married tomorrow, but when Kacey also didn't show up and wasn't in her room, I really began to worry."

"Did you tell Brady that? He might be trying to find Kacey before it's too late."

"I'm not sure, I might have."

"Or he might have overheard your argument, Liz," Pat said. "We need to find them both and sort this out."

"Find the captain and tell him that Kacey and Brady are both missing. Eleanor and I will check below decks to find out if Kacey is in the same place as last time when she was missing. She was let out by someone who works in the engine room."

I took the key out of my pocket and opened the gate that separated lower decks from the one above it. I didn't even think about calling Andrew to tell him what we were doing. All I could think about was finding Kacey before it was too late. Whoever held her wouldn't be all that happy when they found out that she didn't know anything. Right now, I wasn't sure if Brady was involved or not, since he wasn't even on the ship when she went missing the first time, but that didn't mean that someone else on the ship wasn't involved with Kacey's disappearance. I didn't even want to think about how far this plot might have gone.

"Do you think we should really go down there?" Eleanor whispered in my ear.

"We need to hurry."

When we were in the corridor that led to the engine room, it was deadly silent. The only sounds were the creaks and groans of the ship as it broke through the waves of the ocean.

Neither Eleanor nor I spoke right now. I certainly didn't want to alert anyone that we were coming. It eased my mind somewhat that the captain was being alerted.

I began checking all of the closet doors, but Kacey wasn't in any of them. I even checked the closet where we found out she had been held the last time. When the door creaked open, Kacey wasn't there and I lost all hope, until we walked out of the room and heard scuffling along the far wall. I led the way and followed the noise, even though my heart beat louder and louder. Was I heading to my death, or would we be able to save Kacey in time?

Eleanor pulled me backwards and we hid behind part of a wall that extended out enough to remain unseen. Then I heard whimpering and Kacey's voice say, "Keep looking for that money."

"What makes you think it's even down here?"

"Because your father said it was when I called him. He was very obliging when I told him I had you tied up and that your life hangs in the balance if we don't find what we're looking for."

Musical laughter followed. "Smart move, but I'm shocked my father would even care. It's not like we've seen each other the last year."

There was a clanging of metal and grunts of frustration. This certainly was a turn of events. Just when I heard a popping sound and something metal being scrapped across the floor, there was another sound: my cellphone, saying: 'You have message from Andrew.'

I pressed my back against the metal wall, as Eleanor and I tried to move toward the nearest door where we could hide, but no such luck. Suddenly Kacey and Brady confronted us.

"What are you doing down here?" Kacey asked, with a narrowing of her eyes.

"Oh, you know, we made a wrong turn somewhere and wound up down here," Eleanor said with a shrug. "Of all the luck, you're here, too."

"We've been looking for you, you know, to see if you're okay since you went missing, again?" I added.

"We figured that since Brady was also missing, you two might be together. We should leave you alone now. It's none of our business what you're doing down here."

"What do you think, Brady?" Kacey asked.

A pistol was pulled out and Brady pointed it in our direction. "I think that they're lying. I also think they heard every word we said."

"Get in here," Brady said, with a motioning movement of the gun. "Before I shoot you right now."

"Okay, okay," I said. "But with all the metal down here, a bullet might just ricochet and kill you instead of me."

"She means, us," Eleanor said.

"Would you two get moving," Kacey said. "We don't have all night."

"Nope, the captain will be down here soon," I suggested. "Then what will you do?"

"She's right, we can't stay here, Brady. We need to off these two and come back later to search for the money. It's a nice night for a swim, don't you think, ladies?"

"And here we've gone out of our way to help you. I suppose that man from the engine room finding you was set up?"

"No, I was looking for the money, but when I heard someone coming inside, I pretended I was asleep. It worked perfectly, as you can see. You two bought my story pretty quickly."

"So, why did you play dead on our deck?"

"She needed somebody to make her later story make sense. That's why the camera only shows her going down the stairs by herself. There was never anyone who kidnapped her, not even to try and pressure her father to talk," Eleanor said.

"Actually, my father was being a little resistant about telling me where he hid the money after the robbery."

"You were here when it happened?"

"Yes, but when the feds showed up, we knew there was no way that we'd be able to take that money off the ship, so my father hid it."

"A year ago, you mean? What makes you think he didn't have somebody else come back for the money and lie to you about it."

Kacey shook her head. "No, he wouldn't do that. We were partners."

"Money has that effect on people. You just said you haven't spoken to your father in years."

"What was I supposed to say, that I visited my father regularly in prison? I had hoped that one day we could do a job together."

"I guess the apple didn't fall too far from the tree," Eleanor said. "But why choose a life of crime instead of going to college and leading a regular life — like getting married and having babies, like everyone else does?"

"I'm not like everyone else. There's nothing like the thrill of stealing; like when I stole that master key the first day from Officer Barber."

Eleanor rolled her eyes. "That must be the crime of the century."

"Why didn't you come back for that money before now?"

"The FBI was aboard watching this ship for six months. We had to wait until things cooled down. I couldn't risk people knowing that my name was once again on the registry too soon after the robbery. I was the one who recommended the cruise wedding to Liz and told her what ship to take. Liz was pretty easy to convince."

"Yes, but how did you know that she'd ask you to be in her wedding?"

"I sent her flowers and a letter of congratulations, hinting that if she wanted me to take part in her happy day, to just let me know. I knew Liz would eventually give me a call, which she did. The rest was only a matter of setting things up, including telling her how I didn't have the money to pay for the cruise."

"So, you not only used Liz to get on this cruise, but you didn't even want to shell out the money to be here? Or are you that broke?"

"I need this money and when I find it, my dear father isn't seeing a dime of it, since he wouldn't share the location with me. It's about time I branch out on my own."

"Shouldn't we get going, now?" Brady said. "In case the captain really does show up."

"Yes, grab these old bats and we can go up the back stairs."

Brady took ahold of our wrists and we were being dragged through the engine room. I gazed around in a panic, hoping, praying, that somebody would be here who could help us, but it was empty. We were shoved through another door and we were in a small corridor that led up an equally small set of stairs. When we went through the last door at the top, we were on the main deck on the starboard side. There were lights far overhead on a string that tapered down and I could hear the rush of the water as the ship cut through the waves.

I dug in my heels, but it was hopeless, as we were being propelled closer to the handrail. We grabbed it tightly with both hands as we were released and Kacey yelled, "Jump."

"I'm not jumping ship," I said. "If you want a swim, you jump."

"Yes," Eleanor said. "I agree with Agnes, jump, Kacey."

"Brady, would you do something? Toss them overboard."

Brady drew back. "I didn't agree to that. You told me that you'd give me a cut of the money, but we've been looking for hours and it's just not there. I think your father screwed you over here and lied."

"He wouldn't do that to me. He only told you when he thought my life was in danger. The money has to be in that room somewhere."

"Don't listen to her, Brady. I know you need money for medical school, but there has to be a better way. You're marrying into a wealthy family. I'm sure they'll help you out."

"I can't ask them to do that, at least not right away."

"If you want to be a doctor, why would you even involve yourself with a murder of two old ladies? That's quite a bit to live with."

"Don't you see that Kacey is just using you, Brady?" Eleanor said. "She needs the muscle to move things around in that room. Why else do you think she brought you in?"

Brady took a step back now. While I couldn't see his eyes, I was sure that he was giving this some thought.

Kacey took the gun from Brady now and said, "Push them off this ship, or you'll be the one who is dead."

I slapped my head in frustration now. Why did Brady give up the gun so easily?

"Over the side, ladies," Kacey said.

"Better do what she says," Brady said.

"You, too," Kacey hissed between her teeth. "I should have known better than to expect you to be of any help. You're soft and weak."

"And if we won't?" I asked.

"I'll shoot you in the face. Not even your daughter will recognize you at the funeral."

Brady stepped forward. "Don't do this, Kacey. It's over. There is no sense in going to jail for murdering anyone when you can't even find the money."

"We won't tell," Eleanor said. "Or at least, I won't."

I shot Eleanor a look and said, "Please listen to reason. This doesn't have to go down like this."

"I'm not murdering anyone, you're committing suicide. It's known to happen on cruises." She cocked back the gun and ordered us one final time to get over the side. Eleanor and I climbed the handrail, gripping it with death-like holds. I just couldn't believe I'd go down this way and by some girl I had tried to help. My phone rang and I scrambled to answer it, my hands slipping to the last of the rail. I held on for dear life and the next thing that happened was Kacey falling backwards, up and over the rail, sailing to the ocean below.

"Hold on, Agnes," Eleanor shouted.

My hands were too slippery with sweat now and tears trailed down my face as the pounding on the deck could be heard. Two hands reached down and I was pulled to the top of the rail as Andrew helped me the rest of the way over. Brady assisted Eleanor over and onto the deck. Once I was there, I slumped to the deck, clutching a fist over my heart.

"Th-Thanks," is all I could muster to say.

"Woman overboard!" Eleanor shouted.

A lifeboat was lowered and Eleanor raced to my side. "Oh, Agnes, I thought we were a goner for sure this time."

Andrew lowered himself to sit next to me on the other side and took my hand, putting butterfly kisses on my cheeks. "What happened to Kacey?"

"Brady bum rushed her and she fell overboard. You could say he saved our lives," Eleanor said.

I wanted to say that if it wasn't for him, we might not have even been in this predicament in the first place, but I didn't.

"Thanks, Brady. If you hadn't acted when you did, Kacey would have forced us to jump ship."

"I shouldn't have let Kacey talk me into helping her, but I didn't see any harm in helping her look for money hidden on this ship."

"So, that's what this was all about?" Captain Hamilton said.

"Yup, Kacey's father stole the money from Han Smith last year. I'm not exactly sure how involved Kacey was, but she made it sound like she was just as involved in the theft, too."

"Her father told Kacey that he hid the money somewhere on the ship, but wouldn't tell her where," Eleanor added.

"Eleanor is right. That's when the kidnapping plot happened, but the person that let her out of that storage room prevented her from searching like she would have liked, so she played it off like she was drugged and told us that she couldn't remember what happened that day. She even told us that the last thing she did remember was the ship leaving port."

"Since she didn't find the money yet, and she couldn't get her father to tell her where it was, she had me call him and threaten to kill her if he didn't tell," Brady said. "She brought me in when I came aboard, promising to give me a share of the money for school."

"I'm still not understanding why it took an entire year for her to come back to this ship, but she claimed you were watching the passenger lists and the FBI was even watching the ship after the robbery on other cruises."

"Yes, but the money was never located. If the money was ever on this ship, it's long gone by now."

I was helped to stand now. "I could show you where they were searching for the money, Captain."

"I think you've been involved enough already, Agnes," Andrew said.

"Nonsense. Kacey also told us she was the one who stole the master key from Officer Barber."

"Yes, apparently she was honed by her father to lead a life of crime," Eleanor said.

I guided the group below decks as I heard Kacey screaming that Brady had tried to kill her as she was helped back aboard. "You're making a terrible mistake," she went on to say.

"Tell it to the FBI when they arrive," a security officer said.

We descended the stairs that led below decks and this time, I had none of the tension that I felt the last time Eleanor and I came down here. When we walked into the utility closet, I said, "They were trying to move things in here, perhaps the money is behind something."

Shelves were moved and that's when I gazed overhead. "Have you tried checking the light panels?"

"They're screwed closed," Hamilton said, but he barked off orders. With a few minutes a ladder had been retrieved and a man removed the screws that held the light cover and said, "There's nothing up here."

Andrew began inspecting the walls when a squeaky noise was heard. "I think this floor panel is loose."

He stepped away and Captain Hamilton told them to get Ben to check it out. When the officer showed up, he instructed the men how to remove the floor panel and once it was up, they lifted out a large duffle bag. We all stared wide-eyed as the zipper was moved back and the cash was revealed.

"Looks like the money was here the whole time. I'm just not sure why or how," Hamilton said.

"They were doing construction in this room about a year ago," Ben said. "And the area down there was more than big enough to hide a bag this size."

"I don't see why Kacey's father didn't come after the money himself," Eleanor said.

"He expected Kacey to do the dirty work is why. Perhaps the father wanted to see how badly Kacey would go to find the money as a way to prove herself to him," I suggested.

"I guess the feds will figure that out when they take Kacey's father into custody," Hamilton said.

Andrew led Eleanor and me back up to the main deck. Kacey was nowhere to be seen and Brady was being questioned, but he wasn't in handcuffs at all.

When I went over there, I thanked Brady for his help, again. "You're welcome. I've been working undercover for over a year now, looking for that money. This was a pretty big operation," Brady said.

"What? This entire wedding was a hoax?"

"A very deliberate one," Liz said. "Once we had Kacey on our hook, it didn't take long to reel her in, but you can't simply rush a wedding and an entire wedding party. I just hope my parents will forgive me when they find out that there won't be a real wedding."

"But why did you let us look for Kacey and Brady like that?"

"We needed for it to all play out. It wouldn't have worked out nearly as well if we were the ones who went below decks. I knew you'd be able to get a confession on tape much easier once we found out you'd also be on board. I know your son Stuart and he's the one who told us to let you do your thing, that eventually you'd be able to not only figure out what really was going on, but also to get Kacey talking."

"What tape?"

"We hid a recording device in your sandal."

"This is why nobody trusts the government," I said, irritated. "But how did you even know that it would play out like it did?"

"Honestly, we weren't sure, but we're willing to give you a reward for finding the money. Your son insisted upon that."

I shook my head and Andrew's jaw was tight as he said, "It would have been nice if you'd have shared information with us. Agnes and Eleanor almost lost their lives."

"Why didn't you show up to save the day before I almost fell off the ship?" I asked.

"We would have, but we couldn't find you. We thought that you were downstairs, not on the deck," Liz said.

"But what about the tape?" Andrew asked. "That should have helped you."

"It did, but it took longer to find out what part of the deck they were on. I'm sorry it took so long," Liz said.

"If you're an FBI agent, Brady, how did Kacey get your gun away from you so easily?"

"That was totally unexpected. I didn't think she'd do that, I was trying to stall until the other agents got here."

Obviously, Brady needed to brush up on his skills, I thought.

Andrew was quite angry and led Eleanor and me into the atrium, where it was standing room only. Mr. Wilson rolled his scooter forward and Eleanor ran to him, giving him a big hug and kiss.

Captain Hamilton pulled me aside and told me that the hot tub did indeed have an electrical issue that most likely led to the death of Ricky and Leo. I was relieved that Leah hadn't been involved. She had been through enough. I thanked the captain for sharing the information, but kept it to myself. I certainly didn't want to cause him any trouble since he was really very helpful in our case, even if he didn't know it. I also told him how Kacey had stolen the master key from Officer Barber that first day so hopefully the captain would be too mad at him from losing the key.

When she glanced up, Ruby stepped forward. "I'm sorry I caused you any problems, Eleanor. I can see now that you and Mr. Wilson really do love each other. I don't know why I was acting like I did. I'm just a bitter old lonely woman."

"You don't have to be," Eleanor said. "There are plenty of widowers out there, eager for the picking."

The crowd surrounded us, asking for details about how we almost lost our lives bringing down Kacey and finding the money, too, in the process. It was many hours before we were able to get back to our room as every time we tried, party people danced us around the deck until the wee hours of the morning. While I was dead tired after our day, when sunrise came, it was so breathtaking that I wouldn't have wanted to miss it. On the horizon were oranges and yellows as far as the eye could see, and when the sun was rising, it appeared to be coming out of the ocean itself. Andrew came up behind me and slid his arms around me, resting his head on my neck. While I didn't expect to have such an eventful honeymoon, I was certainly on it with the right person. I wasn't sure what tomorrow would hold, but I'd face each of my days wrapped in Andrew's tight embrace.

About the Author

USA Today Bestseller Madison Johns isn't the type of writer who publishes one book a year. She works hard to publish once a month, whether it's one of her beloved Agnes Barton mysteries, or her intriguing paranormal romances under the name of Maddie Foxx. She says that she learned early on while watching other established authors that loyal readers are always hungry for the next book. Therefore, she makes sure never to keep her readers waiting too long for the next story. She burns the midnight oil with a strict publishing schedule, meeting her deadlines at any cost.

An avid animal-lover, Madison hails from mid-Michigan and loves to use her home state in settings for her books whenever possible.

Add your email address to receive new release alerts and get new books for only 99 cents!
http://eepurl.com/4kFsH

Other Books By Madison Johns

An Agnes Barton Senior Sleuth Mystery Series
Armed and Outrageous
Grannies, Guns & Ghosts
Senior Snoops
Trouble in Tawas
Treasure in Tawas
Bigfoot in Tawas

Agnes Barton Paranormal Mystery
Haunted Hijinks
Ghostly Hijinks
Spooky Hijinks

Kimberly Steele Romance Novella (Sweet Romance)
Pretty and Pregnant

An Agnes Barton/Kimberly Steele Cozy Mystery
Pretty, Hip & Dead

A Cajun Cooking Mystery
Target of Death

Lake Forest Witches
Meows, Magic & Murder

Kelly Gray (Stand alone) Sweet Romance
Redneck Romance

Paranormal Romance as Maddie Foxx

Clan of the Werebear
Hidden, Clan of the Werebear (Part One)
Discovered, Clan of the Werebear (Part Two)
Betrayed, Clan of the Werebear (Part Three)

Shadow Creek Shifters
Katlyn: Shadow Creek Shifters (Ménage shifter romance-Book One)
Taken: Shadow Creek Shifters (Ménage Shifter Romance) Book Two
Tessa: Shadow Creek Shifters (Vampire/Werewolf Romance)

Printed in Great Britain
by Amazon